Best
Vegan
Science Fiction & Fantasy

2016

Also from Metaphorosis Books

Score – an SFF symphony

Reading 5X5: Readers' Edition
Reading 5X5: Writers' Edition

Best Vegan Science Fiction & Fantasy
Best Vegan SFF of 2018
Best Vegan SFF of 2017
Best Vegan SFF of 2016

Metaphorosis Magazine
Metaphorosis: Best of 2018
Metaphorosis: Best of 2017
Metaphorosis: Best of 2016

Metaphorosis 2018: The Complete Stories
Metaphorosis 2017: The Complete Stories
Metaphorosis 2016: Nearly Complete Stories

Monthly issues

by B. Morris Allen
Susurrus
Allenthology: Volume I
Tocsin: and other stories
Start with Stones: collected stories
Metaphorosis: a collection of stories

Best Vegan Science Fiction & Fantasy

2016

---

edited by
B. Morris Allen

ISBN: 978-1-64076-900-7 (e-book)
ISBN: 978-1-64076-899-4 (paperback)

from
Metaphorosis Publishing

Neskowin

Contents

From the Editor

One of the great strengths of speculative fiction is right there in the name – speculation. Science fiction and fantasy, in their different ways, push us to think about new ideas, new situations. They encourage us to keep our minds open, to understand that not everyone sees the universe the way we do. Science fiction stories pose problems – current problems, possible ones, unlikely ones – and help us think about we could, would, and can do to solve them. Fantasy stories drop us into worlds with different rules, different histories, different structures. In short, an openness to difference is essential to the genre. There's no point in speculating if you're not ready to look at something new.

Of course, there's another side to science fiction and fantasy – the escapist, entertaining side. Speculative stories take us away from our own quotidian worries, to worlds that are more exciting, more interesting. Even when bad things happen, they're not happening to us, and our heroes usually survive. They give us hope – if this awkward child can escape from the witch, or that grizzled pilot can find happiness in the face of danger, we can escape and find happiness too. Even if things are hard now, the world can change, can get better.

This collection is aimed at both sides of the genre - it's full of stories that will make you look at life in a different way. But it's also designed to take you to a better world – a vegan one, where animals aren't casually eaten or exploited or mistreated. It's a chance to read and explore without skipping the unpleasant parts. These aren't stories *about* veganism. There's no proselytizing, no directed philosophy, no moralizing. They're stories that just happen to *be* vegan.

There's always a place for writing that challenges us, that makes us think hard about our default values, that questions our unquestioned morals. But, frankly, most of us (vegan or not) already spend a lot of time in environments that don't live up to our ideal values. So there's also a place for writing that gives us a break, and let us just relax and enjoy ourselves. If you're vegan, these stories will do that. And if you're not, they're just a lot of fun to read. Either way, have a good time!

B. Morris Allen
Editor

Dedication

For Moses, Rosita, Caribe, Malinche, Grace, Penny,
EBB, Yggdra, Xanthus, and Latska

My Dog is the Constellation
Canis Major

Jarod K. Anderson

I didn't actually want a dog, so I guess I got what I wanted. The little guy belonged to my grandma. I don't know many old ladies, but I still feel confident saying that she was a very cool old lady. She was 85 when she died, but she wasn't that "so old it hurts to look at you" kind of 85 that makes death a blessing. She was more of a "gardening every day, cornerstone of the local astronomy club, post inappropriate jokes on your Facebook" kind of 85. She was also the only family I had left in Ohio, so it was either me or the shelter for her little dog when she died.

I hate to think how things would have been if that dog had gone to a shelter. I wonder what the workers and volunteers would have done when the little guy started to expand like unspooling Christmas lights, impossibly bright, tangled in the shape of dog. It hurts my heart to picture that loving collection of cosmic bodies crouching in a kennel.

I'd tell you the dog's name, but he really didn't have one. Grandma just called him "Dog" or "Big Dog," which I always assumed was a joke because he seemed to be some kind of dachshund Chihuahua mix. He looked a little like an elongated black German shepherd that somebody shrank in the dryer. I asked Grandma where she got him once. She poked a finger skyward and said, "Up there. Made him just for me." At the time, I thought that was an unusually religious answer for her. I should have known better.

Sometimes it doesn't matter how young you are at heart. When your bones are 85, your bones are 85. Grandma fractured her pelvis and both ankles when she fell off her front porch. She had her big telescope set up on a tripod. She had gotten it just where she wanted it and didn't want to move it again to clean some dust off the lenses, so she hung off the front railing to get at it. The wonderful idiot.

The broken bones led to the hospital. The hospital led to pneumonia. The pneumonia did the rest. It was all over in less than two weeks.

It sounds terrible, but I was glad it didn't take longer. When she got sick, she could barely breath. It looked and sounded like it hurt. It also changed the way we talked to one another. She knew she wasn't going to make it back home, so our conversations started to be about important awkward things, the stuff you want to make sure you say to someone before you're gone for good. We talked about loving each other. We talked about the good times we had when my mom was still alive. She tried to tell me about what she'd learned from life, about making meaning for just for yourself, but it wasn't easy for me to hear her and she got tired quickly if she tried to talk too much. Toward the end, she really couldn't speak at all, but from the look in her eye I had the feeling there was a lot more she wished she could tell me.

I thought about grandma's last moments a lot after the dog changed. I thought, "this is what that anxiety behind her eyes meant." I think she would have been proud of me. I didn't scream or lose my mind. The change happened when I was ready for it. Because I was ready for it.

I missed our old conversations, the ones punctuated by stupid jokes and grandmas pseudo-spiritual science lectures. She loved astronomy, loved it like some old people love Jesus and she spoke about it in that same tone. It was reverence. She would talk about things light-years away. About the careful balance of forces that kept us from spinning off into the great, frozen nothingness that hemmed us in on all sides. As she spoke, her voice would get low and solemn like somebody reading a bit of scripture in a Sunday service. There was real passion in it. Then, once I felt small and weightless, like a strand of her silver hair rising up and away, like a bit of cobweb caught in the breeze, then she would pause for a moment. She would look me square in the eye and say, "And you're part of that. Part of the same tremendous machinery that does all that. Not one bit less amazing. You and me, sitting here trying to puzzle it all out in our own heads. It's important work. It means something."

She'd drop all that in my lap one minute, then walk around the corner into the kitchen and make fake farting sounds the next. I'd hear her giggling and I'd play along saying, "Grandma! What did you eat?" I lived with that amazing woman on and off from age 15 to 26. So, the question of whether or not I would keep her dog after she passed was really no question at all. That dog was like grandma's family. So he was my family too.

Plus, since I ended up inheriting grandma's house, it was more like I was moving in with the dog, than he was moving in with me. He liked me well enough. I sorta always viewed him as my replacement. He arrived just after I moved out, about four years before grandma passed. I didn't know much about dogs, but it wasn't hard to tell that he was glad I was there. Honestly, I was just as happy not to be alone.

I hired an auction company to come in and sell off a lot of grandma's things, but I kept the important stuff: old pictures, her journals and notes, many of her books, and of course her big telescope. I even toyed with the notion of joining the astronomy club. At first, I just set up her telescope on the front porch and tinkered with it. I had no clue what I was looking at, but it was still pretty cool to have a little peephole into space. From there, I decided that a proper tribute to my grandma's memory would involve putting some effort into stargazing, so I began cracking her books and journals. I'm glad I did. Otherwise, I probably wouldn't have had any idea what to think when Big Dog started to grow into his name.

Most of grandma's journal entries were about astronomy. She would write about what she could see on a given date and how it compared to her expectations from consulting her astronomy books. On the first night she got a good, clear view of Saturn you'd think she'd won the lottery. The page was tearstained. There were also lots of notes and sketches about the constellations, but not all the entries were pure astronomy. Some of them read more like philosophy.

The word "subjectivity" kept showing up in entries. See, grandma believed that there was no "inherent meaning" in the universe. Nothing meant anything by itself. Some people might think that's kind of a grim, sad idea, but not grandma. She saw it more as a job opening. People could make meaning and meaning needed made.

She often used the constellations as an example. There was nothing about the relationship of certain stars that made them into a ram or a crab or a dipper. We made them into those things. People. Staring up into the night sky and giving things names, giving them meaning and relationships to one another. She didn't think of this as just interesting or fun. She thought of it as a power and a responsibility. Human beings were the things in creation that could give names and meaning to the incredible mechanisms of existence.

When I read those sorts of journal entries, it was like I was fifteen again, feeling small and impossibly big all at the same time. Orion didn't look like a hunter because of the suggestion of ancient astronomers. Orion *was* a hunter because of the *decision* of ancient astronomers and that power was just as real and important as the force of gravity. Those sorts of ideas, written in my grandma's thin, looping script, made me absolutely dizzy.

Sometimes, after staying up late reading grandma's journals, I could have really used a good fart joke. I had to settle for dog snuggles instead. Dog snuggles, warm and fuzzy, it turns out, are a good cure for most problems, physical or philosophical.

Grandma's philosophies were haunting me on the day I understood her dog. I had never owned a dog before, but I still knew that he wasn't always very doggish. Sure, he loved walks. He loved treats. He loved to snuggle on the couch. But he also loved sitting in front of the window at night and staring off into the sky. He would even look up at the ceiling or down at the floor, sometimes for more than an hour, slowly turning his head as if he was tracking the movement of things I couldn't see. It was a little creepy at the time.

All of the dog's oddities and grandma's ideas were swirling around my head on the evening I picked up an old book on constellations and finally came to the section on Canis Major. The Great Hound. The Big Dog. I looked down at the furry little guy next to me and I understood –and when I understood, I swear to you the dog actually cocked his head. It was like an acknowledgement. Like he had been waiting for me to understand.

That's when everything started to change. Grandma really truly believed that the meaning we make ourselves is the realest meaning there is. That's how she understood life and, somehow, it's how she could understand the constellation Canis Major as her own little furry companion.

I believe that my grandma was right about the world. It's hard not to believe after what I've seen. Even so, I'm not her. When I understood what Big Dog really was, he couldn't be a dog anymore. I couldn't make him be a dog anymore.

He started to grow. That first night, when I first understood, he must have grown almost a foot. More than that, he started to glow. Not a lot. Not at first. I could barely see it until I turned out the lights for bed and even then it was just a faint outline, a shimmer.

I called off work. I closed all the blinds. I decided I wouldn't leave the dog's side.

That was the start of it, but he changed faster as the days passed. A few days later, he was the size of a Great Dane and it wasn't just a general glow anymore. There were actual points of light and, thanks to grandma's books, I had names for those points of light: Wezen, Adhara, Murzim. And of course there was Sirius, the dog star, right in the center of his chest like a gleaming celestial heart.

The bigger and brighter he became, the more ridiculous I felt about continuing our usual dog care activities, but when he scratched at the back door, I wasn't about to tell him he couldn't go out to pee. I was a little nervous about it. Grandma had a big wooden fence around her back yard, but you could still see into it from the neighbors' second floor windows. Sure, the neighbors were elderly, but Big Dog was looking more and more like a walking, pony-sized, light show. He was hard to miss.

Even stranger than the light, as he grew I could start to see the space between the stars in my dog. I thought I could even see the circling swirl of nearly imperceptible dust, the whir of planets and other interstellar bodies moving in concert with the stars that made up my puppy. If I looked too long or too closely, I started to feel both massive and distant, like I was no longer standing on firm ground. If I looked too long, I felt downright nauseated.

A week after I understood, Big Dog was the size of a bear and he had no fur left to stroke. Touching him felt like dipping my hand in freezing water that carried a mild electrical current. He was a field of lights, a cloud of gleaming motes with the defining stars of his constellation burning so brightly it was difficult to sleep near him at night. But somehow, he was still a dog. He still paced back and forth on the living room rug. He wagged a tail of cosmic light and unknowable distance when I looked at him or said his name. He was still my dog.

On that last day, I woke up from an evening nap to a dog-shaped cosmos bigger than a grizzly sitting at the foot of my bed and staring out the window. The blinds were pulled, but that didn't seem to matter. I sat up and sighed. His big head swung towards me, a canine shaped wedge of space. I could hear his big tail thumping on the hardwood floor and I thought Sirius, the heart of my dog, shone out a little brighter when he turned toward me.

I got up, rubbed the sleep from my eyes, and headed toward the front door. I hadn't opened that door since I had first read about Canis Major. My dog followed me, casting blue gold light that filled the house and threw strange shadows from the lamps and furniture onto the walls. The dog was the only light in the house and his presence made all the usual, domestic objects seem like a landscape fit for giants on a universal scale. I felt like a titan of nature, a thing that breathed and walked through the universe like a child strolling through a toy train set.

When I reached the door I turned to face my dog. There was a lot I wanted to say. Important things. That was the meaning I wanted to make. I thought for a while, listening to that "thump, thump, thump" of tail hitting floor. In the end, I only got out one word.

"Thanks," I said.

I decided it was enough. I opened the front door and stepped aside.

Big Dog walked up next to me. He was so big he had to stoop to fit under the ceiling. He stopped and lowered his head so that he was eye level with me. In his face I saw a view of the cosmos with eyes magnitudes upon magnitudes larger than my own. I was bigger than solar systems. I could see the movement of stars and planets in relation to one another. I felt more than saw the intricacies of gravity and matter and energy all moving and shifting in a pattern so complex that it, for a moment, seemed simple. It was beautiful.

A lump rose in my throat and I wasn't big anymore. I felt small and unanchored again, just like when my grandma spoke about space in her church voice. I was without time or place. I was without significance.

Then, that big, beautiful dog took a step forward and licked my entire face in one slobbery motion. It felt like getting slapped with both the cold of deep space and the heat of undiluted starlight. It also felt wet and more than a little ridiculous. I laughed so hard tears ran down my cheeks. I laughed and smiled up at that brilliant interstellar puppy grin and I was home again.

Canis Major ducked down and somehow wriggled through the front door and out into the night. I raised my arm to my mouth and blew out a raspberry fart noise on the back of my forearm as he stepped down off the porch. It was the best way I could think of to honor my grandma and the dog that brightened her twilight years. Two steps out into the yard, he was bigger than a house. One step more and he blended into the night sky, fading from view, but the shake of his shoulders as he went told me he was laughing. At least, I decided he was laughing.

I did end up joining the astronomy club after all. I like to think grandma would be proud of me. I'm trying to be as curious and, well, weird as she was, but it's a pretty tall order. These days, I'm particularly fond of studying the constellation Draco. In practical terms, it might be tough to actually have a pet Dragon, but on the other hand I've become less and less concerned with what's practical.

There are nights, though, when I just need some simple companionship. On those nights, I look for Sirius right at the heart of my fury friend. Then, if I can get his attention, a see a tail wag that sweeps across the sky of the southern hemisphere. I still have a lot to learn about the constellations, but I do know one thing. Canis Major is a very good dog.

"My Dog is the Constellation Canis Major" originally appeared in *Metaphorosis* on Friday, 8 July 2016.

About the author

Jarod K. Anderson's fiction and poetry has been published in Asimov's, Daily Science Fiction, Apex Magazine, and elsewhere. Jarod lives with his wife Leslie in Ohio in a house full of books, comics, and the happy sounds of dogs racing from room to room.

You can find out more at www.jarodkanderson.com and follow him on Twitter @JarodAnderson

Images Across a Shattered Sea

Stewart C. Baker

The air on the cliffs above the Shattered Sea was hot as a furnace and twice as dry. Still, Driss couldn't suppress a shiver at the way the shimmering message-globe moved through the sky, dozens of meters above the churning, black waves.

He had seen the globes before, of course, but only after they'd been captured and put on display in the village's cozy museum. It didn't quite seem real, the way the little ball bobbed and danced on the breeze, drifting ever so slowly towards Fatima where she stood atop a heap of boulders at the edge of the cliff.

"Here it comes," she said, waving her net back and forth as she hopped from foot to foot.

Her eagerness just made the dangers of the place worse. It was as if she didn't care that one misstep would send her tumbling to her death. Driss himself would have been happy never to have seen the coast in person. It had always been a deadly, desolate place, even in the days when the message-globes blew across the sea in huge clouds which blotted out the sun. And those days were long since past: They had seen only three globes during their two week hike, and this was the first that had come anywhere near them.

"Gotcha!" Fatima leapt into the air, hooking the bubble-like ball in her net and pulling it down from the sky. "What do you think is in it?"

She clambered down from the rock, looking for all the world like a goat rushing down from an argan tree after eating the last of its fruits. Driss laughed at the absurdity of the image, the tension flowing from him as she moved away from the cliff edge.

"A book of law?" she continued, ignoring his laughter. "Perhaps philosophy? Machine schematics? An encyclopedia?"

"A recipe for pie," Driss countered. "A picture of a cat and a joke that makes no sense. Lewd sexual acts."

For all of these, as well, had been found in the message-globes. Driss's father, who had lived through the mad rush to the coast when they first appeared, still spoke with derision of the women and men who had bragged that they would recover the priceless lore of the past, only to find themselves the owners of meaningless trivia.

Fatima *tsk*ed as she sat on a rock. "You have no romance, Driss. No soul. Even those are treasures, to have travelled so long and so far."

"Activate it, then. Let us see what 'treasure' has come to us across time's yawning chasm."

"You are as eager as I am," she replied, waving the globe in its net. "Just admit it, and I'll open it here, where you can be the first to see."

Driss crossed his arms. "Kha! Didn't I come with you on this fool's hike? Didn't I leave a steady job with my father to chase down meaningless messages from a dead civilization? Of course I am as eager as you!"

Fatima grinned and set her catch on the rock.

Up close, the globe looked much sturdier than it had when drifting through the sky. Its surface, which shimmered with the translucence of soap bubbles when viewed from afar, had taken on the sheen of polished glass, or of the mirrored pieces sometimes found in the old, abandoned tunnels to the south. The structure of the thing was not what it seemed, either; far from being smooth, it was made up of hundreds of tiny hexagons, each adjoined to the other in a pattern that shifted subtly as it crossed the message-globe's surface.

As solid as it was, the globe clearly wanted to be off; it bobbed at the top of Fatima's net, held to earth grudgingly at best.

"It's so beautiful," she murmured. "Let's see ..." She flipped the net over and took the globe in her hands, twisting the top portion around so it popped open with a click to reveal a palm-sized grey square. "There."

A small red light flashed, and then the square in the globe's centre came alive, showing not information from the past, but an image of Driss and Fatima in miniature, echoing their expressions and movements in jerky fits and starts.

In the dimness of the panops room, a solitary monitor flickered to life, bathing Jen's face in a sickly, stop-motion glare. She sucked in her breath and pushed a buzzer, then passed several minutes by staring at the scene on the monitor, which showed two people who did not yet exist having a discussion about events that had not yet happened.

The door to the room opened and a man in a beige suit entered. "Whaddawe got, kid?" he asked, clicking the door softly shut behind him.

In the sanctity of her own head, Jen bristled. *I have a PhD in quantum mechanics,* she wanted to say, *and one in electrical engineering. I am not a 'kid.'* But these were not the sorts of thing one said to the man directly responsible for funding one's research, even if he was a jumped-up bureaucrat with delusions of being a general from a World War II movie.

Besides, he'd called her 'kid' so many times now it barely offended. In revenge, she referred to him as *hog* in her thoughts. Hog for his sideburns. Hog for his chauvinism. Hog for the way his eyes narrowed in concentration every time she tried to explain how the panoptic shards worked.

Hog leaned up against the next console over. The smell of his stale sweat, insufficiently masked by strong cologne, wafted towards Jen, making her wrinkle her nose. "So who are they?" he asked. "You picked somebody important, right? The descendants of one of their kings or somethin'?"

Jen sighed. "That's not how it works. The panoptic shard can only broadcast what it happens to find—we can send it to a general place and time, but we can't target it at specific hypothetical individuals."

Hog did the eye thing.

Funding, Jen thought. *Remember the funding.* "Even if we don't know who these two are," she continued, "their appearance and the way they act can tell us plenty about the state of society two hundred years from now. For example, we can assume from the fact that they were able to activate the shard that they have at least a basic understanding of technology. And we can see that the surface is liveable, given that they're not wearing any kind of breathing device or other protection.

"It's very general information—certainly not the sort of thing a market analyst would want to know—but since we're only interested in generalities, it serves our purpose well. And because the images we see in the shards derive in part from the actions we take in the short term, we can use them as a sort of gauge to measure those actions' effects."

"So I map out where we're gonna bomb, and this'll show me how far back into the Stone Age we knock 'em?"

Jen winced. "That's a gross oversimplification. There are so many variables that we can't definitively say a chosen military action alone is responsible for what we see. Even our observation itself causes variation with these people's hypothetical 'control state'."

"What?"

"Think of it like measuring the temperature in a room. If you send someone in with a digital thermometer, both the person and the thermometer are going to add a small amount of heat. And the shards are very sophisticated pieces of equipment—especially given that we've tried to disguise the ones that transmit by putting them in groups of shards which act only as information packets. The mere fact that we've sent them will have impacted the course of future events."

Hog grunted. "But planning a military action *will* have some observable effect?"

"It should, yes."

"Then I'll leave the 'hypotheticals' to you, Kid," Hog said with a grim smile. He jabbed one finger at the screen. "Give me a live stream of this in the situation room. I got meetings to hold."

Then he left, clicking the door shut behind him, leaving Jen alone with the light of the monitor, which showed the silent images of two people she feared she had killed long before they ever had a chance to be born.

Brightness. Heat. The bone-deep sense that something was wrong.

Fatima staggered across a landscape her body insisted was not what she saw, a splitting pain in her head and a hard, silvery ball clutched in one white-knuckled hand.

The ball was important, that much she knew, but the how and the why of it she couldn't quite grasp. And what had driven her to leave the safety of their shelter in the caverns? She had lived there all her life and never felt the need to see the festering, ruined surface world.

A misstep sent a jolt through her brain, and her vision exploded with silver-white sparks. Somehow, she managed to hang on to consciousness, head spinning, until the pain faded and her vision cleared, and then she stumbled to a seat on the steps of a ruined hut near a hissing stream which stank of burning hair. A yellowing skull rested against some stunted lumber which had fallen into the waters, and she wondered briefly who its owner had been, whether she would meet the same fate.

The pressure of the ball against the muscles of her hand was a throbbing counter-point to the thudding in her head. She glanced down at it, away from the skull and the stream. What was it? She had a vague idea that it was what was wrong, somehow. But all it showed was a picture of her, with her eyes scrunched up tight against the brightness of the surface sky, and with several layers of fabric around her face to stop the poisoned air from choking her.

She wondered if she'd been out too long. If the vapours were making her paranoid.

But no. There *was* something out of place. Something she couldn't spot, yet which was as persistent as the throbbing in her temples and palms.

Fatima lay back and closed her eyes, hiding the sun's bloated orb behind the crook of one arm. She needed to rest. She needed to remember.

*

Jen shivered as the woman on screen drifted into a fitful sleep.

If the local environment was any indicator of the average global condition, most of the planet was an irradiated waste. *And all this in only two hundred years,* she thought with a glance to the door. *What in the hell are they planning?*

Jen had always realized, intellectually speaking, that the military wasn't exactly going to use the panoptic shards to make the world a happy place. She'd tried to tell herself that even if they used it to kill people, the technologies she could develop would serve the greater good in the longer term. That she needed the funding. That the ends justified the means.

But this was too much. She pushed her chair back from the console and pressed her fingers against her eyelids until she saw spots, then let out a long, slow breath. She thought of her generation's children, working so hard for what they believed in. They deserved better than this, and the woman and man she'd seen on screen did, too. Everybody did.

She licked her lips, gave the door another nervous glance, and—before she could change her mind—severed the shard's connection.

It was warm in the café, but the kind of warm that was tempered just enough by breezes from the nearby ocean to be pleasant instead of stifling.

Driss sat at a table with Fatima near one glittering window, breathing in fragrant steam from a cerami-steel cup of boiling hot tea.

The panoptic shard with its recording device lay nestled in the centre of the table. Fatima had attached a jamming device and nanocarbon tether, then opened a virt-screen from the terminal on her wrist. As Driss looked on, she scrolled through reams and reams of data.

"It's astounding," she said, pausing to take a hasty sip of her tea. "We've known about the shards for decades now, but this is the first we've retrieved that definitively acts as a transmitter."

Driss nodded. "Makes you wonder if they've figured out we know how it works."

"Mm."

He couldn't tell if she meant it in agreement or if she'd found something interesting, but her pupils had that half-dilated look of a woman focused one hundred percent on her virt-screen, and he knew better than to interrupt Fatima when she got like that. Instead of saying anything more, he went to the counter and ordered a bowl of olives. When he returned, Fatima had moved from reading to writing, her fingers a blur across a projected keyboard.

"Sending them a message?" Driss asked.

"Not quite. Take a look." She flipped the screen his way.

Driss popped an olive in his mouth as he skimmed what she had typed—line after line of equations, algorithms, and other, more arcane code. "All I see," he had to admit after a few seconds, "is a bunch of stuff I don't understand."

Fatima rolled her eyes and unflipped the screen. "You ought to apply yourself more," she said as she resumed typing. "They offer free classes in all sorts of things at Cadi Ayyad. Even poetry, if you're not into the sciences."

Driss spat out a seed and fished another olive from the bowl. "Maybe I'll check it out sometime. But, come on, don't taunt me! What's on the screen?"

"Okay, okay. Given where the shards originate, I highly doubt the senders' intentions are good. They're probably trying to get an edge in one of those unsuccessful 21st-century genocides. There's a signature in their programming which matches what we know about recon and intel work in—"

Driss waved his hands. "Spare me the tech-speak. I won't understand it anyway."

She grinned. "Basically, they're trying to use images of us to change our reality by altering the actions they take against us. So I'm giving them an image. Just ... not the kind they're expecting. And after that, well ...” She made a few final keystrokes and flipped the screen his way again. “Look.”

Driss glanced at what she'd done and let out a low whistle.

Jen flinched as the door slammed open and Hog stormed in, then she went back to pretending she was hard at work trying to regain the connection. In reality, she'd used the time since her act of sabotage to copy all her research onto a secured solid-state drive that now nestled in her coat pocket.

“Get it back,” Hog growled. “Now.”

“I'm trying, sir. So far as our system is concerned, we haven't even lost the connection. It insists we're getting images broadcast like before. I don't know what ...”

She trailed off, jaw slackening, as the monitors that lined the walls flickered on, each showing images of ruined buildings and poisonous landscapes. The console was alive with data, reporting hundreds of activated shards. “*All* of them?” she muttered, tapping away at the keyboard. “But we only have one transmitter. Unless they somehow figured out how to—”

“Oh my dear sweet Jesus.”

Jen's heart skipped at the whispered reverence in Hog's voice. Then she looked again at the images on the monitor. A satellite image of Florida, barely visible beneath a frothing Atlantic. The Eiffel Tower, half-collapsed across a ruined city barely recognizable as Paris. The Vatican afire, bodies strewn from windows and across its many steps.

“What did you do?” Hog asked.

Jen shook her head, but before she could respond —before she could repeat that she had no idea, that this shouldn't even be possible—the screens all flickered off and on again. Only this time, the screens all showed a single image: a timer, set to twenty minutes and counting down.

Hog looked her way, eyes wide. "Turn it off," he said, his voice hoarse.

Jen swallowed. The console was still streaming with data. Hands shaking, she entered the de-activation sequence—and was not much surprised when it failed to work. "I'm locked out," she whispered. "I'm sorry."

Hog didn't say a word. He just turned away and walked through the door, pale and insubstantial as a ghost.

As soon as he was gone, Jen grabbed her coat and ran. It wasn't until she got outside and halfway to the Metro station that the adrenaline poured out of her in one big rush that left her shaky and weak; she had to stagger to a bench before she fell.

She sat back, eyes closed, breathing in the crispness of the early spring day, listening to people's murmured conversations as they dined on the patio of a nearby bar, to the swish of cars and buses driving past. The city smelled of rain, with a hint of the Japanese cherries that dotted the park across the street from where she'd stopped.

In her mind, she kept playing back that final image: those numbers counting slowly, irreversibly down. She wanted to scream, to yell, to run through the city like a mad prophet, warning of the coming destruction. But what would be the point? They couldn't stop it—not now.

A muffled cheer rang out from inside, and Jen opened her eyes. She could just make out some sort of sports game on the T.V. above the bar. Still shaky, she let out a long, ragged breath. Maybe, she thought, there would still be time to have a drink or two before it happened.

She stood to go inside, then froze when she saw, out of the corner of her eye, a telltale glint of a panoptic shard in the sky above the park.

A shard. Not a weapon!

Had she misunderstood the message? It didn't seem likely, with the images the future people had sent. But even just the tiniest hope of it made her heart beat fast and her shakiness vanish. She dashed across the street, dodging traffic, keeping one eye on the tiny mirrored ball as it drifted below the tree line and came to rest in the fronds of a sumac bush.

She picked it out and activated it, and her mouth went dry. Pages and pages and pages of text describing fantastical technologies scrolled past, complete with diagrams and instructions on how to construct them. One was a machine that, as near as she could figure, would establish a real-time audiovisual link between the future and the past.

And there were more, some of which she couldn't even understand. She was standing there, stunned, wondering how they'd targeted her so precisely, when there was a gentle bump on the top of her head. She reached up and retrieved a second shard, which she opened with shaking hands to find an identical payload.

Heart hammering, she looked out across the city. Hundreds more of the bubble-like objects were drifting westward, some landing on empty tables in street-side cafés while others made it into open windows or the up-stretched hands of pedestrians.

They hadn't targeted her. Of course they hadn't: they didn't even know she existed. Instead, they'd delivered an instant revolution to everyone around the world. Hog and his ilk wouldn't know what hit them; they'd be so busy dealing with the consequences of this that they'd never get around to wasting resources on some hypothetical future reality.

She set one of the shards on the path, where it would be easily found, and headed off for home, laughing for the sheer joy of it. Above her, the skies streamed with glimmering secrets, coming down to earth from somewhere far away.

"Images Across a Shattered Sea" originally appeared in *Writers of the Future* on Friday, 4 March 2016

About the author

Stewart C Baker is an academic librarian, speculative fiction writer, and occasional haikuist. His fiction has appeared in Writers of the Future, Nature, Galaxy's Edge, and Flash Fiction Online, among other places. Stewart was born in England, has lived in South Carolina, Japan, and California (in that order), and currently resides in Oregon with his family-although if anyone asks, he'll usually say he's from the Internet.

You can find out more at infomancy.net and follow him on Twitter @stewartcbaker

Rowboat

K. G. Anderson

I've never seen an ocean, but I grew up playing "Rowboat" in my family's cramped living module on level C of Xinxin Colony. The worn blue carpet was the water, the concrete floor beyond it, a sandy shore. With a broomstick as an oar, I pretended I was Gramma Jen, rowing hard against the tide to get us home.

"They'd restricted travel by then, but Gramma Jen wanted us to know about beaches and the sea," Mom said. "One afternoon we found an abandoned rowboat and she took us out on San Francisco Bay. A government patrol nearly caught us."

Mom paused. Sitting in a faded chair, propped up by a thin pillow, she looked exhausted. Dad had told me she'd be gone in a matter of days. Like many of the colony's pioneers, she'd ignored the dangers of radiation to build our station on Ceres.

I closed my eyes, as if that would shut out the sour air of the sickroom. Then I finished the story Mom had told me so many times when I was a kid. The one that had always been my favorite.

"Gramma Jen hid the boat behind an abandoned freighter," I whispered. "By the time the patrol passed, the tide had turned against you. But she rowed you back to shore and beached the boat just as the sun went down."

When I opened my eyes, Mom was nodding.

"Thank you, Maya. I hope you'll always remember that story. Remember Gramma Jen."

With time running out, Mom was telling us all the stories again. How she'd volunteered to come to Ceres on an Early Migration mission. How our Gramma Jen had encouraged her every step of the way.

"Your Grampa Peter didn't want me to go, but she told him she believed I had it in me to be a pioneer," Mom said.

My half-sib, Dad and CeCe's son Rikki, 10 in Earth years, was hearing some of the Gramma Jen stories for the first time.

"So, did Maya's," Rikki hesitated, looking for a word we didn't use much on Ceres, "—did Maya's *grandmother* want to someday live here with us?"

Rikki was playing soldiers on the floor using my old "armies" of hex nuts and bolts. He sounded doubtful.

Mom and the other pioneers were the only ones who talked about Earth. Our teachers always told us to focus on the future.

"Rikki, there was a time when we thought we'd finish all the asteroid colonies in time for our families on Earth to Migrate," Mom said. "And, maybe we could have. But no one expected the Last War—or at least how terrible the Last War would be. Everyone who stayed on Earth, including Maya's grandmother and grandfather, died."

Rikki shrugged and went back to advancing a line of hex nuts toward a regiment of bolts. I knew how he felt. In spite of Mom's stories, and the pictures they showed us in school, for those of us born on Ceres so much of the Earth stuff seemed unreal.

At Earth-16, I was long past my days of playing "Rowboat." I'd moved from my family's living module into the First Gen dorms, five levels down. The Xinxin families had agreed that their children should be weaned away from them, taught to focus on the long-term survival of the colony, and prepared to be assigned to other colonies on other asteroids. We'd form families and have children there. My assignment could come any day now, as soon as the next freighter arrived. My throat tightened when I thought about how I'd never see Ceres, or my family, again.

Mom was asking Rikki a question about school.

I wanted to tell her that I dreamed about Gramma Jen and Grampa Peter. My battered tablet had a copy of the one picture we had of them, taken when they were only a few years older than me. I look at the picture almost every night. In it, they wore the bright, sleek clothing of the 2070s. They were picnicking with friends in a park. She, dark and lively; he, tall and thin. A bridge—the "Golden Gate," Mom called it—spanned the sparkling blue water behind them. I'd seen it in Earth movies.

In my dreams, I was Jen's best friend. We drove a vehicle, a car, with the windows open, across the Golden Gate Bridge, the blue water rippling below, and green forests rising beyond. Because of Mom's stories I could imagine it all: Trees. Oceans. Rain. Earth gravity. The wonders of atmosphere. I smiled to feel the pull of Earth all the way out here on Ceres, tugging me towards the planet where my parents and CeCe had been born.

But Earth wasn't just millions of miles away. Thanks to the Last War, everything on it was rubble. The Earth they showed us in pictures and videos existed only in my dreams.

Voices from the living room told me that Dad and CeCe were back. Rikki jumped up and ran out to greet them. Mom had drifted off to sleep.

I could hardly stand to look at her, slumped in her chair. I knew she was getting weaker. I'd heard CeCe say she'd reached the point where there were more bad days than good. Yesterday a glass bottle filled with a pale green liquid had appeared on in our refrigerator, labeled with Mom's name. I'd changed the subject after CeCe told me what it was. Mom would be confronting death as fearlessly as she'd confronted everything else. She expected us to, as well. I didn't dare disappoint her.

A hesitant knock on the bedroom door. Another one of the pioneers wanted to say goodbye. Edison Kang and I nodded a silent greeting as we exchanged places. I tried not to shudder as his arm brushed against me.

Mr. Kang had many of the early signs of radiation sickness—limp gray hair, creased and wrinkled skin, and ugly lesions. I dropped my gaze. Raised in the safety of the Xinxin compound, I could not imagine him and Mom working for years on the asteroid's surface in the original flexsuits. But they had. All to make Xinxin our home.

That night I dreamed I was rowing a boat through space, searching for a shore. Earth shone bright in the vast emptiness, impossibly far away. I had to get there—Grandma Jen was waiting for me.

I woke soaked in sweat and burning with curiosity.

After morning classes I went looking for Mikel Clark. Mikel was smart, but not well liked or trusted. I usually avoided him, but I'd overheard him bragging about hacking into the inter-colony databases and I knew he'd be eager to show off his skills.

"Is it true they've found more Earth data?" I asked.

Mikel's eyes lit up. He pulled me into an alcove where we wouldn't be overheard. "Two of the other colonies had it all along. They weren't sharing. But now the Xinxin Council has it." He grinned. "The security guys haven't opened up general access yet, they say they have to 'review' it, but people like me can get around that."

"I want to look for some images. Family stuff. Nothing classified."

Mikel flipped his braid over his shoulder.

"You came to the right man. I could get you in through a workstation in the admin section," he boasted.

"Tonight?" I swallowed hard. I'd never broken the rules before.

Mikel glanced down for a moment, as if weighing the risks. "Sure, why not?"

That night I followed Mikel through a maze of hallways. He used someone else's override codes on the doors. We were leaving tracks, but someone else would get blamed. By the time we entered the cramped office deep in the admin sector, I felt sick to my stomach. But it was too late to stop now. Mikel pulled an old data pad from a drawer, connected it to the system, and attached my data card that held the image of Grandma Jen and Grampa Peter.

Sure enough, Xinxin Colony's network now had the Earth archives we had been told were lost or held in secret by one of the other colonies. With Mikel's help, I searched several of the databases with facial recognition software. My first hit was a low-res image of Grampa Peter. He was older—handsome but worried looking. Just as Mom had said, he'd been an official in a California city called Palo Alto. But the matches for Gramma Jen's face were an Elisabeth Washington, a music professor in Georgia. I frowned. I was pretty sure Georgia was nowhere near Palo Alto.

Where was Gramma Jen? I searched for Grampa Peter's name plus "Jen," "Jennifer," and "Jeanne." Nothing. Real estate data from Palo Alto paired his name with a Margaret Dempster. His sister? His mother?

Mikel fidgeted at my side, not as confident as he'd seemed before.

When I typed in "Margaret Dempster," a news story appeared. I saw the words "arson conviction."

Before I could read more, an orange bar flashed at the top of the data screen. Mikel grabbed my arm.

"We gotta go. We've been spotted."

In the distance, an alarm shrilled.

Mikel yanked out my data card, logged out of the pad, and shoved it back in the drawer. Following him as he retraced our path, I saw him toss my data card into the corner of a dark stairwell—figuring, I guess, that I'd be the one blamed for the break-in. I stopped to snatch up the card and nearly missed catching the door he'd keyed open. I'd been stupid to trust Mikel.

Sure enough, there was trouble.

"You went looking for Gramma Jen."

It wasn't a question. Mom beckoned to me from her narrow bed.

"I'm sorry."

Mikel and I had been caught on the admin network and they'd told not just Dad, but Mom. I'd hoped I'd find something to make me feel better, but all I'd done was make my mother feel worse.

"I'm sorry," I said again.

"No, Maya," Mom said. "It's my fault."

My eyes went wide. This didn't sound like my mother.

"I hoped you'd never find out," she said. "So many records were lost in the Migrations and the War. But I guess they're finding some of that data can be recovered. I should have told you."

"Mom, I didn't find anything," I lied. "Just a picture of Grampa Peter from his job."

Mom gave a clipped laugh, devoid of humor. She reached for a cup of tea from the bedside table and took a sip. I watched her trembling hand and tried not to show my confusion.

"Maya, you didn't find anything because there's nothing to find. There is no Gramma Jen. Never was."

"*What?*"

Mom, sitting on the edge of her narrow bed, flinched.

"If there's no Gramma Jen..." my mind spun with possibilities. Was I adopted? "But you're still my mother?"

She reached out her thin arms and I knelt beside the bed to be hugged.

"Oh, Maya, of course I'm your mother."

Relief poured through me. After a minute I felt Mom square her shoulders. I settled cross-legged on the floor and waited, shivering. Mom was getting ready to tell me—once again—that things weren't as frightening as they sounded.

"Maya, I invented Gramma Jen. I need to tell you why."

Mom hugged herself as if she were cold. I reached for a blanket to cover her, but she waved me away.

"I'm afraid the story starts with Margaret Dempster," Mom began.

"She was my..." she stopped, worked her lips, and continued. "She was the woman people would say is my mother."

Her tone turned as grim as I'd ever heard it; my stomach twinged. Margaret Dempster, the arsonist, was my grandmother?

"Margaret was ..." Mom sighed and shook her head, casting about for words. "I know now that she was mentally ill, but when I was a child, all I knew is that my brother and I seemed to get punished no matter what we did and my father...well, he loved us but he just couldn't admit that there was anything wrong. He couldn't protect us. We left home as soon as we finished high school."

"I thought that simply by coming to Ceres—as far away as anyone could get during the first Migration—I'd solved my problems," Mom said. "And, in a sense, I had. Our work building Xinxin was important—far more important than anything I could have done on Earth. I met CeCe and your father, we all were in love, and—Maya, we were so happy."

A smile lit her face and eyes.

"I don't think you can even imagine what our lives were like," she went on. The smile faded.

"Then, the Last War—only six days, but when it ended, everyone on Earth was gone and we were alone in space: six colonies on three asteroids. Two of the colonies failed—one from starvation."

I nodded. They'd told us this, over and over again, in school. But what did this have to do with Gramma Jen?

"We were focused on mining, agriculture, manufacturing, and production of everything we needed to survive—including children. With no more Migrations from Earth, it became crucial for the colonies to have children before we got too much radiation. That's when I began to have nightmares. I dreamed that I'd had a baby and when I took the baby in my arms, I turned into Margaret. I dreamed that I hated my baby. Once I dreamed that I ... was lighting a fire."

I shuddered. Mom didn't know that I knew about the arson. Tears rolled down her skeletal cheeks. Her head fell forward. Her thin, lesioned hands covered her face, then fell to her lap.

"Maya, I would wake up from those dreams knowing that something was terribly wrong with me. My friends were having children. They loved those children! I saw Edison Kang holding Leah when she was born, and I couldn't imagine ever feeling like that. I was a sick, broken person. I didn't want anyone to find out."

I turned my head so Mom wouldn't see the tears rolling down my cheeks. "Mom, why didn't Grampa Peter help you? Why didn't he divorce her and take you away?"

"Maya, I've asked myself those questions a thousand times. We'll never know."

Mom put her ravaged hand on my arm and gently shook it, as if to wake me up.

"Let me tell you about the picture."

Mom stretched out her hand for the battered data tablet on the table by her bed. I handed it to her, and with a few taps she brought up that picture of the young couple at the Golden Gate, the two I thought of as Gramma Jen and Grampa Peter. I stared at the striking young woman. *Elisabeth Washington.*

"This photo saved me," Mom said. "I found it in a digital album my dad had given me years before, when I left Earth. I'd never bothered to look at it. I thought he'd given me a lot of images of nature and landscapes, in case I never came back."

"After the Last War, when it was all gone—then, of course, I looked at the album. I came across this picture, recognized him, and I looked at the metadata. It was taken in 2071, two years before he married Margaret. I realized that my father had wanted me to know about that beautiful moment in his life. He wanted to send that woman, whoever she was, with me into the future."

I sat on the bed beside Mom and saw the picture as I never had before. The woman looking at the camera while Grampa Peter held her hand and gazed at her as if she were the most precious thing in his world. What had happened to separate them?

"That's Elisabeth," I said. "Mom, I found her."

Mom frowned.

"I found her. Facial-recognition software. She's Elisabeth Washington. She taught music in Georgia. What do you know about her?"

I'd thought I knew all Mom's stories, but now there was so much more to know and so little time left.

"Elisabeth…" Mom stared at the picture and shook her head. Then she dropped the tablet onto the bed and lay against her pillow.

"Maya, all I know was that my father had loved her. When I saw that picture I realized I could rewrite history, for him and for me. I could make *her* my mother. The mother I'd always wanted. A wonderful mother.

"I named her Jen after the neighbor who'd given me the art lessons Margaret refused to pay for and who told me I had talent. Her courage came from the ship captain who mentored me on the First Migration. Her generosity is from CeCe. I got all those great recipes—and the story of the rowboat—from Nina, my first roommate on Xinxin."

While Mom told the story, my dad and CeCe had slipped into the small room. Dad caught sight of the tablet with the photo of Grampa Peter and Gramma Jen.

"Gramma Jen is one of your mother's finest creations," he said, sitting carefully on the bed beside Mom.

So he had known. Mom leaned her fragile body against him. Her dark eyes were bright with tears.

"Maya, for me, your Gramma Jen was not just real —she was essential," Mom said. "She changed my life. She made yours possible."

The room spun. I didn't know what to think. Gramma Jen had become a stranger. My real grandmother—I opened my mouth to ask about the fire. But I closed it again. Mom was falling asleep. I tried to slip out of the room, but CeCe stopped me.

"Maya…tomorrow," she whispered, squeezing my hand.

I pulled away, mumbling that I needed to study for an exam. That was true, but instead I took the long way through the corridors that led back to the dorm. I walked close to the grimy, familiar walls, afraid that the artificial gravity I'd grown up trusting might prove as unreliable as my ties to Earth. Fearing, as I never had before, the cold and airless world where I'd been born.

The next evening, my mother asked for the injection. With all of us gathered in the room and a recording of her favorite Beethoven sonata playing, Dad slipped a hypodermic into a vein. She took three, perhaps four, shallow breaths and then Mom was gone.

We gathered again a few days later, to watch as her ashes, wrapped in fragile Earth-made fabric, were taken out onto the frozen surface of Ceres and placed in the colony's communal grave for pioneers.

"Maya, you can refuse," Dad said. "I asked them not to tell you about this when your mom was so ill.

He sat on the bench beside me, looking over my shoulder as I opened the tablet and read the message.

I gasped. They were offering me a permanent assignment to Charboneau Colony on Vesta. This was out of the blue. I'd always thought they'd send me to Pallas or Hygiea, never imagining I'd qualify for the agricultural engineering team at Charboneau.

"Mom would have been thrilled." I felt tears start to well, but shook them away.

"I think it's too soon for you," Dad said. "But the freighter will be packed and ready to go by the end of the week. And this is the closest Ceres will be to Vesta for 17 years."

I nodded, my eyes fixed on the message. Permanent assignment. Charboneau. I'd have only three days to pack and say goodbye to Dad, and CeCe, and Rikki and nearly everyone I knew on Xinxin. Three of us from Xinxin First Gen would leave on the freighter *Sunrise* and travel 930 million miles to join the agricultural engineering team at Charboneau. We'd live on Vesta for the rest of our lives.

I thought of Mom again. She'd left Earth to build the first colonies. She'd understand. And Gramma Jen. She'd...but there was no Gramma Jen. Confused, I shook my head. So I think it surprised Dad when I turned my face to him and said "I'll go."

The words sounded so small, so flat and empty. But once I said them they set in motion a whole new story.

Dad and I hugged without words.

I walked slowly back to the dorm, trying to imagine my life on Vesta. Living with strangers—and eventually creating a family with some of them. New foods. A new religious system—some of the parents were worried about that. A quasi-military system of government, stricter than the democracy we'd maintained in Xinxin. I frowned as I recalled that data access on Vesta was rumored to be far less liberal than on Ceres. If I wanted to find out more about Elisabeth or Margaret, I'd have to do it now.

To my surprise, Dad got me official access to the Earth files. I read the news story I'd glimpsed before —"Palo Alto Woman Convicted of Arson." Margaret Dempster had set her family's house on fire. Everyone had escaped unharmed. A small, blurry photo showed a pale, frightened woman. To my relief, she looked nothing like my mom.

I would never know why Grampa Peter had married her. But now I understood why my mother had replaced the broken world of her childhood with the fantasy of Gramma Jen.

I found real estate records for Elisabeth Washington in Atlanta, Georgia, and a review of a concert performance. One of the pieces she'd played I recognized as Mom's favorite Beethoven sonata. I pressed my fingertips to the screen, as if I could reinforce that connection between the two of them—but it was as thin and as wishful as my own ties to Earth.

Had Elisabeth Washington married? Had children? My searches came up empty. I knew as much as I would ever know.

The inside cabin Leah, Jinx and I were assigned on the *Sunrise* proved to be cramped and stuffy, the bunks narrow and hard. We complained at great length that first night so none of us would be tempted to talk about home and the families and friends we were leaving. At last I crawled under the thin blankets, exhausted, but too excited to sleep.

I thought of Mom, and the many times she'd soothed me to sleep with her stories. In the dark cabin, I began to tell my own tale.

Like Gramma Jen, I'm rowing a boat. I'm not alone. There are people in the boat with me. My friends. And someday, my children. I envision a small boy and an even smaller girl, their faces pale with worry, who sit facing me, their hands gripping the seat.

To pass the time I tell them stories of Ceres and Earth and their families, both real and fantastic.

I feel the polished wood of oars against my palms. Each stroke I take sends the light of the stars around us rippling through the black of space.

"Almost home," I murmured as I drifted off to sleep. "Almost home. I'll get you there."

"Rowboat" originally appeared in *Metaphorosis* on Friday, 12 February 2016.

About the author

K.G. Anderson is a Seattle-based journalist, arts reviewer, humor columnist, and technology writer. She worked on the launch of Apple's iTunes Music Store, wrote a book about the iPhone, and served as president of the board of

Northwest Folklife. She shares a house full of books and cats with bookseller Tom Whitmore and lives for the warm summer months and gardening.

You can find out more at writerway.com/fiction-by-k-g-anderson and follow her on Twitter @WriterWay

Daughter of the Sea

George Nikolopoulos

Magdalena could swim before she could walk. She could hum the songs of the sea before she could speak. When she cried, her tears were the salt of the ocean.

She didn't remember her mother. Years ago, a storm had swept her father to the shores of Galaxidi, baby Magdalena in his arms. Father had sailed all over the seven seas, but he never set foot on a boat again after that. A carpenter now, he wouldn't stop talking about the sea — and yet, in all the stories he told, he never once mentioned her mother or the shipwreck. Whenever Magdalena asked him, he just grew silent, until she finally learned not to ask.

Magdalena's father raised her in the busy sea-port of Galaxidi, with stories of the youssouri, the haunted tree that lives at the bottom of the sea, feeding on the fools who dive and try to cut it; of Gorgona, the sister of Alexander the Great, who catches passing ships with her tail to ask the sailors if King Alexander still lives; of Asaf, the giant Arab who can drink up the ocean and clog the seas with his mighty black beard.

She grew to become a young woman. She was beautiful, but boys shied away from her. Perhaps it was her big grey eyes that changed color according to her moods, just like the sea.

Magdalena loved her father; still, when she was sixteen, she ran away from home to become a sailor. Girls were not allowed to be sailors, and so she cut her long black hair and walked to the port of Itea, along the way stealing a boy's clothes while he was swimming. She found employment as a deckhand on the first ship she saw at the port. The ship's name was "Panayia Spiliani;" her own was Michalios, she told the first mate.

As Magdalena's ship sailed across the Aegean Sea during her first voyage, the sky turned black, and thunder started rolling. Soon, the waves were like hills and the small ship was thrown here and there like a nutshell tossed about in a winter storm.

They reached the eye of the storm, and there they beheld Gorgona; Magdalena knew her as soon as she laid eyes on her. She was tall as a mountain; her hair was black, her face beautiful and proud. Below her bare breasts, she had the scales of a fish and the tail of a sea-serpent, long and sinuous.

Gorgona fixed her eyes on the seamen, scrutinizing them. She was terrible and magnificent, and her eyes were like the sea, wise and angry and beautiful beyond reason.

The ship's captain, Kapetan-Giannis Gavalos, was an old sea wolf who knew all there was to know about Gorgona. He'd never met her himself — but back when *he* had been a young deckhand, he'd served under a captain who had faced Gorgona and lived to tell the tale.

Kapetan-Giannis waited for the inevitable question, but, to his astonishment, it never came. In all the tales he'd ever heard, Gorgona had hastened to ask "Does King Alexander still live?" But now she just kept staring at them, silent, terrible wrath blazing in the edges of her eyes. In the end, Kapetan-Giannis decided there was no point in waiting any longer, and he had to take the matter into his own hands.

"O Mighty Gorgona," he shouted above the howling of the wind, "King Alexander lives, and he reigns, and he rules the world." Trembling, he confronted her with an expression as solemn as he could manage.

She grew terrible to behold. Her eyes burned, her voice was like a thunderstorm.

"*Liar!*" she shouted. "I know that my brother is dead and has been so for two thousand years. All captains had lied, but my mortal lover told me of his death. For years I grieved, yet in the end I came to accept it.

"Then I realized that while I was lost in my grief, the wretch had left me, and he had taken my daughter with him. I want my daughter back! Tell me where she is or I will sink your ship and drown you all!"

Ashen-faced, the captain looked at her. "I don't know where your daughter is, Gorgona. I didn't even know you have a daughter!"

"Liar!" She shouted. "All men are liars."

She coiled her tail around the ship and started to squeeze. Timbers started to creak, ready to break apart.

A wild impulse seized Magdalena. While the ship rocked and swayed, she began to climb the main mast. Many times she almost fell, as the mast, along with the ship, was jerked around, but she held on and inch by inch she managed to climb upwards.

"Hey, Michalio!" shouted the seamen from below. "Are you crazy? You're going to fall to your death!" But she finally made it to the crow's nest on top of the mast.

Magdalena could look at Gorgona eye to eye now. "Spare the men, Gorgona!" she shouted. Then, "please," she whispered.

Gorgona laughed. "Why should I spare them, boy? All men are liars, like the one who said he loved me and stole my daughter from me." She squeezed harder.

The crow's nest swayed like a willow in the wind, but the girl held fast. She stared at Gorgona's angry eyes. They were grey like her own.

Silently, Magdalena started to take off her clothes; she took them off one by one, until she stood naked on the crow's nest. The seamen stared and shouted in amazement, but Magdalena had only eyes for Gorgona. "Take *me*, mother," she shouted, and she jumped off the mast into the water.

The men of "Panayia Spiliani" swear that when the sea became calm again there was no sign of Gorgona or the strange girl who had been Michalios.

All around the Aegean Sea, sailors still tell the tale of Gorgona's daughter, though no one knows her name.

Only an old man in Galaxidi knows. He used to be a carpenter, but now you can always find him in the tavern, drowning himself in his drink.

"Daughter of the Sea" originally appeared in *Truancy* on Monday, 26 December 2016

About the Author

George Nikolopoulos is a speculative fiction writer from Athens, Greece, and a member of Codex Writers' Group. His short stories have been published in *Galaxy's Edge, Grievous Angel, Helios Quarterly, Unsung Stories, Bards & Sages Quarterly, SF Comet, Mad Scientist Journal, Truancy, Digital QuickFic, StarShipSofa, Antipodean SF, Manawaker Studio's FFP*, and many other magazines and anthologies.

You can find out more at georgenikolopoulos.wordpress.com and follow him on Twitter @g_nikolop

Tides of Reflection

Mark Rookyard

The winds whispered promises of winter as they plucked with cold fingers at Silven's shawl. She held it tighter around her shoulders and tucked her hair behind her ear. It was quiet on the cliff tops, the world seemingly shocked into appalled silence after the violence of the storm the night before. The sky was a parched blue, and diamonds of light danced on the sea under hazy pink clouds.

The path along the clifftop was overgrown, the grass thick and yellow. Once, the sea had been crowded with laughter and play, Silven watching from these very cliffs, afraid of the depths, unable to swim. Now the sea was quiet and undisturbed, the laughter long forgotten.

Below her, the waves were secretive and quiet, red near the pebbled beach, but growing darker out past the island with its alien walkways of impossibly ancient orange stone. Far overhead, plumes of white smoke trailing behind it, a scutter flew. More colonists free to flee now the storm was over. The raging winds could only keep them here for so long.

A small figure worked on a beach scoured clean by the winds and the rains. It could only be Jerek. It seemed to be a matter of honour to him not to be beaten into hiding by the presence of the sea.

Fear and frustration made Silven bold. She pulled a stalk of grass and twined it around her fingers as she strolled down to the beach. Jerek didn't look up from his work. Curls of wood littered the pebbles around his feet as he ran a plane over the bottom of an upturned boat. His boots were thick and worn.

After a long pause, as the plane scraped and the sea murmured, Silven finally said, "You're making another boat?"

"Aye," Jerek said. The hair on his chin was coarse and dark. He shook splinters of wood from his plane.

Silven watched him until the sun was low in the sky and the sea was hunched and whispering and dark, retreating from the beach. Taking its secrets with it. Taking Kal with it. She held her shawl tighter. Jerek was wiping the bottom of the boat with a rag soaked in something thick and oily.

"We have something in common, you and I," she said finally.

The rag stopped its circular motions a moment, only a moment, before it continued. "Aye," Jerek said. "You, me, and a score of other people in this forsaken place."

The wind whispered and the clouds drifted and the sun sank in the sky.

Silven turned to watch the sea skulk away like some furtive, sated predator. Kal was there, in its depths. It took her breath away to think of it. To think how cold it must be. How dark.

She left Jerek to his boat, alone and defiant under the cold stare of the sea. She could hear his hammer all the way as she walked back up the cliffs.

Marus was home when Silven returned. He sat at the kitchen table turning a small plaque around and around in his hand.

Silven switched on a light and opened the fridge.

"Where have you been?"

Even though she was looking in the fridge, Silven knew Marus hadn't turned to ask his question.

"The beach." She took a bottle and sat at the table, not looking at Marus.

"The beach." Marus smiled, looking at the plaque in his hand. "We couldn't drag you there before and now you can't keep away."

"Jerek was there, making another boat."

Marus nodded, turning the plaque around in his hands. "He's always been one for the sea. Even now, he can't change what he is."

Silven thought she knew what that plaque was, and it made her heart ache and her throat tighten at the sight of it. "What's that you have there?" She had to fight to keep the anger from her voice.

Marus put the plaque on the table. 'Kal's Room' it said on it. There was a picture of a dog, black and white. "We have to see to his room," Marus said.

Silven felt her face flush. "Can't you wait? Are you so ready to be rid of him? You won't even go to the beach now! Why are you so keen to forget your son?" Her voice was shrill and she had to fight to catch her breath.

Marus was calm, sitting there, his fingers never leaving that plaque, and Silven hated him all the more for it.

"I was the one who took him there, Silven. I taught him to swim in those waters. Don't you think I hate myself for it? I feel it too, you know. I can feel what lured him out there. Oh, you're safe from it. Using your fear as an excuse, surrendering to it. Now you're free to judge me, condemn me." His fist was white around the plaque.

"Yes, you were the one to take him out there, weren't you?" Silven's anger was cold, her breath even, though she knew her hands were shaking as she slammed the door of the habitat behind her.

The cliffs were dark out towards the coast, the alien towers quiet as they watched the silent sea beyond.

She wondered if Jerek would be out there, facing the grim sea alone.

Silven had been watching Jerek work on the boat for most of the morning. She sat on a large rock and the wind blew in her hair. Jerek hadn't said a word to her.

"You're not afraid," Silven said, relenting. "Most are afraid of the sea, yet you still go out there." The sea was gentle before them, pale red as it lapped against the pebbled beach and the forgotten jetty.

Jerek looked up at her. He'd cut his hand, the wound raw and untreated. "Out there?" he said.

"Yes," Silven said. "Isn't that why you build the boat? To take it out to sea?"

"Aye," Jerek had to allow. "That is what boats are for." He sighed and ran his hand along the side of the boat. Its bow was smooth and angular, almost looking as though it had been shaped from a single piece of wood. It was big enough for two people, Silven noticed, and couldn't help wondering who Jerek would ever take with him now his wife was gone.

"Don't you hate it?" she said, her voice unnaturally loud over the eternal wind.

Jerek looked up from his work, an eyebrow raised. "Hate it?"

"The sea. It took your wife," Silven said. She wanted to hurt him, to see pain in his impassive face, though she couldn't have said why. Only two years before, he and his wife had been guests at Silven's habitat. He'd looked younger, then. Happier.

"Aye, that it did." Jerek picked up a dirty rag to wipe his hands. Blood smeared on the stained cloth. "My Lisen, your Kal, and a score of others, it took."

Silven felt tears sting her eyes. "I used to hate her. Your wife." She remembered Lisen at her habitat, pretty and full of smiles.

Jerek grunted and looked at his boat with a practiced eye.

"She was with Kal when he should have had his mother with him. She was where I should have been," Silven persisted.

"There's more out there than my wife and your son."

The wind was stronger now. Thin clouds wisped high in the sky, and the red sea rippled against the jetty legs, warped and bent and skeletal. In the distance, bowed trees leaned sorrowfully, thin leaves brushing the roofs of long-abandoned cabins, doors askew and windows empty.

There had been a time when the beach here was always crowded, full of laughter and hope. Boats had been plentiful in the sea, and in the distance, the island and its ancient walkways had been busy with play. The colonists had loved playing on that alien stone, orange under the red sun. They had run along its walkways, criss-crossing above the water, sometimes ten hands high and sometimes barely breaking the surface of the sea. The walkways were narrow, and the children had turned it into a balancing game, trying to stay on the stone without tumbling into the water.

Silven had always stayed away. The sea had filled her with fear even before it had taken her son. It spread to the horizon like some ancient secretive god. How could anything be so giant, so powerful? Entire worlds could fit into its depths and still not come close to its surface.

"She told me she wanted a son, once. At my habitat, when you and Marus had gone out for a smoke. She was so excited, thinking of all the generations to follow her here on this new world."

"Did she?" Jerek looked at Silven, his face tanned beneath the thick hair lining his chin. She hadn't noticed the creases around his eyes before. "She never told me that." He looked back at his boat, though not with the same intensity as before.

"I suppose we all had our dreams, coming here." Silven fell silent and listened to the sea breeze. She imagined Kal whispering in that wind, whispering that he loved her, that he forgave her.

"Why do you come here?"

Silven opened her eyes. She hadn't realized she'd closed them. Something dark flashed in Jerek's eye as he looked at her. Until he asked her, she hadn't known the answer. Now she did. "I come here because you don't hide. You don't try and forget."

Jerek smiled and there was only bitterness in it. "I don't believe you," he said. "You want your son. You want to join him." The wind rippled in his thick dark hair.

"It doesn't call to me." Silven blinked away angry tears. "It doesn't sing to me. Why Kal and Lisen? Even Marus. Is there something wrong with me?"

There was no answer from Jerek. He was already back to working on his boat.

Silven remembered her first Rirshon. There had been music then, and laughter and banners. There must have been a thousand people there to celebrate the alien tower casting its brilliant white light over the sea. Now there were perhaps a hundred, huddled into their coats, around the base of the great tower.

"You didn't have to come, Marus," she said, looking at the tower. Once a year the sun would shine just so, to catch the great jewel in the top of the alien tower. Its light would be refracted out over the sea, a great searchlight starting in the west and slowly moving east until it cast its piercing glow over the island and its alien walkways, turning the orange stone a blazing red.

Marus' face was pale from the cold, his nose red. "No, no, I wanted to come. I know you think this is important." His hands were stuffed in his pockets. Years ago, he would have held her against the cold.

All around them, other colonists gathered, some sitting on the steps of the tower, others leaning against the wall of white stone, barely any of them showing interest in the light of the tower cast out to the distant sea.

Jerek wasn't here, Silven had noticed. She wondered if it meant anything that she had bothered to look for him. She wondered if it meant anything that he hadn't bothered to come to the Rirshon.

"Dena and Sten came to see me the other day." Marus watched the blazing white light from above as he spoke. A cool wind blew in his fair hair. "They said they're booked on a scutter next week and that there's a place for us if we want it. To Litoka." Still he didn't dare look at her. The light from the tower turned the red waves a pale dusky pink.

"Oh?" Silven kept her voice deliberately monotone. She watched the light. Watched the sea. The waves were quiet, the sea thoughtful in a gentle breeze. "And what did you say to that?"

Now Marus did look at her. His blue eyes were rimmed with dark circles. "I said I'd speak to you, obviously."

"What's so obvious about it?" Silven struggled to keep her voice down. "You'd leave this place? Leave Kal?" She took a breath. Dione and Sal had walked to the edge of the cliff, talking quietly together as the light of the tower played on the waves in the distance. "You go if you want. Leave me here with our son."

Marus turned to face her, and for a moment Silven thought he might touch her, hold her, even. She wondered what she'd do if he did. The possibility seemed as incomprehensible as the alien tower with its fantastic light behind them.

"That's what worries me, Silven," Marus said, his hands remaining firmly in his pockets. "You don't feel the lure of the sea, I know. Otherwise you wouldn't go down to the beach like you do. You wouldn't want it, Silven. It's like an ache in my heart. It pulls at my very soul."

"But why do you feel it and not me?" Silven said, wondering if the bitter jealousy showed in her face.

"I think a lot of us feel it," Marus said, his lips white, his eyes tired. "There's something cursed here, Silven. We should leave while we can." He looked up at the great tower above them, its brilliant white light searching the waves below. "Did you ever think of the ancients? What happened to them? Why are they no longer here? Did the sea take them too?"

"But if you feel it, why are you still here?" It was only as the words were out of Silven's mouth and hanging on the cold sea breeze, that she realized the cruelty of the question.

Marus only smiled, his eyes faded and blue. "For you, Silven. For any love you still might have for me. Because I hate to think of you alone. I can fight it for all those things, if I must."

Silven watched the alien light probing the red depths of the great sea and wondered if Marus knew that he was no comfort to her at all. How could he be, when the very sight of him reminded her so painfully of Kal? The same blue eyes, the same nervous smile.

She knew she should say something, say how much she needed Marus, how lost she would be without him, but she couldn't form the words. The love and the words were lost to her as though the sea had taken them and enfolded them in its cold dark depths.

Instead she said nothing and together they listened to the wind and the waves far below.

"Don't you ever feel it?" Silven wondered. She sat with her legs stretched before her on a warm stone before the sea. The wind whipped her hair and she tucked her skirts beneath her legs. She hated the question, hated the blandness of it, but still she wanted to know what Jerek thought.

"Feel what?" Jerek had pushed the boat into the lapping red waves. He lashed the rope around the jetty. The boat bobbed and rocked. There was something fascinating in seeing Jerek stand in the dread sea, standing there proud and brave, the fearful water turning his trousers dark.

Silven pushed her hair away from her face. She knew what she must look like, sitting there with her legs before her, her hair blowing and the wind rippling in her clothes. She saw Jerek's silences and indifference almost as a challenge to her womanhood, he seemed so unconcerned by her presence. It was liberating to think of herself as a woman, as anything other than a bereft mother. "The lure of the sea. Doesn't it ever call to you?"

Jerek shrugged. "Would I still be here if it did?" He strode out of the water and sat next to her, the droplets of water bright in his dark hair. "Look, what do you want of me?" Jerek spread his large hands and the wind ruffled the collar of his shirt. "You can come with me if you like, in the boat. Come to the island. Though I can tell you there are no answers there to find."

Silven felt a brief flush of hatred then. She hated his strength and his dry eyes. She hated how he could face his past and his loss and not hide from it. She hated him because she realized how afraid she was. She could quieten this fear, she now realized, clutch it to her breast and suffocate it. What was there to fear when she had already lost everything? She got to her feet.

Jerek hesitated only a moment before he followed her to the boat. He got in first, holding the boat steady with braced feet as he helped her in with a hand.

She could see the pebbles shimmering beneath the surface, some pale as eggs and others many-coloured. She trailed her fingers in the water and closed her eyes. Should she hate the sea? Or should she love it? This was Kal's home now. Had these very waves kissed his skin, caressed him the way they caressed her own fingers at this very moment?

Jerek was quiet as he rowed and Silven closed her eyes against the sun. She listened to the wind and the water. What had Kal heard that lured him to the depths? What had Lisen and the others heard? Silven tried to turn the whispering of the sea into promises, words of love, but all she could hear was the sighing of the wind and the cry of the blue-winged birds above. 'Flee!' they almost seemed to cry. 'Flee! Fly!'

Silven opened her eyes to watch them circle overhead, dive into the depths and then return to their nests in the green-fringed cliffs. Had they watched Kal slip into the sea? Had they told him to flee, to turn away? Silven watched the ganwings, white-bodied and blue-winged, circle and circle, and wondered what they had seen, whom they had watched walk into the waves, never to be seen again.

And whom would they tell? Whom could they tell? Would they even now watch Jerek row them far out from shore, row and row until the waves swallowed them? Whom would the birds tell their story to?

Silven looked from sky to sea, her fingers still trailing in the water. She saw fish no larger than her little finger, dark and large-eyed, darting this way and that, mouths opening and closing like silent sinners praying for divine intervention.

Jerek's hut looked small and alone back on the shore. The cabins further along the beach broken and empty, doors askew and roofs already falling into ruin, paint blistered and peeling. Silven remembered Kal changing in those cabins, running out into the sea laughing, his body thin and pale under the red sun. Had it really been so long ago?

Out here the sea was deeper, a darker red. It sloshed against the bow of the boat, the waves thick and slow. Jerek rowed and rowed, with more effort now, his shoulders bunching.

How deep was the water now? Deep enough to have engulfed Kal? It was colder here. She imagined slipping from the boat, falling into the red depths, joining Kal and crying out into the silent darkness. "I'm here! I'm here for you, Kal!" She imagined reaching out, taking him in her arms, their hair flying about them like grass in the breeze.

Was the water talking to her? Putting these thoughts in her mind, seducing her like some persistent lover? She shook her head: it was only her idle dreams she saw.

"You see anything?" Jerek asked, still rowing. "You see any answers down there?"

Silven didn't answer. She watched the sun, low on the horizon, a burning ball of red. She watched the clouds, thin and fine as lace, trace across the sky. She watched the ganwings circling and circling, crying out, mournful and lost.

Who was to say the answer lay in the sea? Perhaps it was in the sky, in the air, something hovering there, calling out to the lost, telling them to give themselves to the waves?

No, Silven shook her head. Looking out at the vast expanse of red before her, quiet as glass towards the horizon, it spread for as far as the eye could see. The answer lay here. The ancients had known this, that's why they'd built their walkways in the water, and had their lights casting about the red waves.

Jerek rowed with more purpose now. Leaning forward and then back. He looked like some great captain facing the dark. Not like Marus, hiding from the memory of his son, hiding from the lure of the sea.

"You see it?" Jerek said, nodding with a jerk of his head.

The island was a green expanse of land lying on the flat redness of the sea. A cluster of trees grew there, flowering vines hanging from the crooked branches. And the vines grew from the island itself, trailing in the sea like quivering fingers. The island shifted with the tide, swaying this way and that, but seemed to be anchored by the walkways made of stone burnished orange in the dying sun. They spread for perhaps twenty lengths out into the sea, still bright even after all these years, even with the sea lapping and licking against them.

The vines trailing from the trees rippled in the wind and the grass shivered on the island as the birds overhead cried and cried.

The island, once Jerek had lashed the boat to the pier, shifted under their feet. It was soft like sponge and seemed to roll with the waves. The vines hanging from the trees smelled cool and bright and Silven wondered if Jerek had once brought Lisen here.

She touched the warm stone of the pier and wondered what ancients' hands had made this place, or if they'd had hands at all. The stone seemed to glow with an inner light. Where the water touched the pier above the surface, it seemed to hurry away in drops and pools, as though eager to be back into the vast expanse of the sea.

The rails were low around the walkways, around the height of Silven's knee and she imagined a childish master race, scuttling this way and that, short-legged and bright-eyed, playing in the waves. Playing as Kal had once done. Laughing.

All around the cool winds blew and the sea whispered and the stone thrummed with warmth. Had Kal sat on this alien platform and let his thin legs dangle in the water? If only she could have seen it! The need of it took her breath away.

"Here," Jerek said. He stood farther out into the water, the sea lapping against his feet and the ancient walkway he stood on. The railing was higher there, the stone twisted and shaped into something that reminded her of the vines hanging from the trees. "This is why I come here." Jerek waited for her to come to him and then pulled a slice of bread from his pocket, tearing a crust off and then throwing it into the water. He leaned on the railing, smiling. "Look."

Silven fell to her knees next to him. Colours coiled in the water, reds, and blues and greens, muted by the redness of the sea, until the iridescent scales broke the surface as a score of fish came to eat the bread. The fish were as large as Silven's arm, sleek and fast, graceful in the water, their lips thick and their fins fine as lace. Their eyes were large and black, dark as the antennae on their backs were bright. Their fins rippled as they fought for the bread. "They're changing colour," she whispered as she watched them.

"Aye," Jerek said. He threw some more bread in the water, and glistening scales broke the surface as the fish turned and chased the food, barging into each other, scales now orange and red and purple, bright and lovely in the waning light of the day. "See how those colours change with their mood?"

Jerek threw more bread into the water, leaning on the railing, watching them turn from green to red to blue, flashing and darting in the water. "These are the young. The giants are out there," he gestured to the horizon spread before them where the waves were quiet, the sea dark. "The giants live out there in the deep. I've heard they change more than their colour." Jerek broke off some more bread and smiled at her, something broken and bitter in his smile.

The sea spread before them, infinite in its vastness, red and quiet and still under a blue sky. She imagined giant creatures out there in the silent depths, imbibing the memories of the sea. Perhaps the sea remembered monsters from the past, or children from the present...

Silven watched Jerek throw the bread. He smiled as the fish turned and turned around the pier, sometimes brushing against the alien stone, their black eyes searching, and their scales red and yellow and purple. Sometimes their antennae would glow white, sometimes gold.

"These young are always here," Jerek said. "Always waiting for me when I come to feed them. The giants only come to shelter under the roots of this island when the storms chase them from the deep." Jerek looked younger, talking like this, more like the man she remembered from those long ago dinners at her habitat. He had talked about his work then, his eyes had been bright and he had held Lisen's hand under the table.

She touched his cheek, and met his eyes when he looked at her. He smiled and took her hand, led her back to the island and they lay under a tree where the vines shook and rippled and the leaves were a parched yellow.

There was something hurt in Jerek's dark eyes as he looked at her, and when he touched her face, her neck and breasts, there was a desperate anger there. He made love with the same desperation, angry and fast, Silven's skirts pushed up around her waist, and when he came, he cried out his wife's name with a desperate sob.

They lay next to each other, looking up into the vines and listening to the wind rippling the waves. Bitter tears stung Silven's eyes as she watched the leaves in the darkness. She said nothing, Jerek's breathing rapid next to her. She couldn't bear to listen to it. She got to her feet, pulling her skirts down, and went to the pier. The clouds were white against a red-tinged night and the sea quiet as it rolled and rippled.

The fish were quieter now, with no food to fight for. They circled in the water, dark and silent, sleek as eels. And somewhere out there in the dark depths, the giants waited, remembering.

⁂

"The Grayson boy's getting better." Marus chewed with effort, his chin working.

Silven watched him. She'd thought him so clever when they first met. "Is he?" She tried not to remember Jerek's angry lovemaking, the way his beard had scratched her cheek. The desperate cry of his wife's name.

"Yes. It was touch and go for a while. The fever's broken, though. Garen and Bel were relieved, obviously."

Good for Garen and Bel. Happy parents. Relieved parents. Silven looked at her plate. Plena again, the vegetable thick and white.

"So," Marus dabbed at his lips with a napkin. "So, that was quite a storm last night. I was worried about you here alone through it."

The habitat had rocked in the wind, the windows buckling under the violence of it. Silven had gone out to the cliffs in the darkness, the clouds thick and broiling, the trees bending, the waves far below frothing and furious, curling up and crashing down against the beach in great swathes. She had watched the sea, her hair whipping about her face, thinking of the dark giants of the depths stirring under the fury of the waves.

"It's kind of invigorating," Silven said. "Being alone. What's to fear when you're alone?"

⁂

The beach was fresh, scoured clean by the violence of the waves. The air hummed with the memory of the storm. And Jerek wasn't there.

Scutters skimmed overhead in the clear sky and there beneath the shelter of the cliffs, the cabins had been savaged by the storm. Roofs were ripped, doors destroyed. Once this colony was no more, what would there be to remind anybody that man had been here? That Kal had been here? She could see the twisted alien tower, bright and gleaming. The pier at the island, that would still be unmarked by the storm, she knew.

But where was Jerek? His boat was there, overturned in the middle of the beach, its side scratched and scraped. She remembered the pain in his cry: 'Lisen!' and she felt shamed at the memory. She had thought him strong and brave, but he was no braver than Marus, no stronger than Marus. And she had been no stronger than either of them, giving herself to him. She remembered the look of regret in his eyes as he rolled away from her, the look of loss. Had he given himself to the sea? His hut was empty, the oars leaning against the wall, bundled together with frayed rope.

The boat scraped and bounced along the pebbles as she pushed it into the water, gasping with the effort. She soaked her skirts climbing into it, through waves lazy after their efforts of the night before. Would the giants already have returned to the deep? She rowed, biting her lip in determination. The waves felt thick and slow in resistance, but still she rowed.

The sea was quiet at the island, almost as though it was shocked at its own fury. Silven walked around the matrix of the pier, her skirts trailing in the water all around her. She sat on the walkway, her arms on the railing, and let her legs dangle in the water warm on her skin.

They came, coiling and spiralling, flashing scales breaking the glass-like water, and then sinking again. They were blue, red, green and every colour in between. The fish nibbled on her legs with cold lips, their antennae flashing white and gold, spinning in the ripples.

She saw it then, a shadow, deep and rising through the flashing fish. It was large, perhaps as large as Silven herself. She leaned over her knees to look closer. It came through the smaller fish, this shadow, dark as the night. She blinked, and then blinked again. She recognized the sombre eyes first, and then the narrow nose. He looked peaceful, his dark hair flowing about him. Jerek smiled, not a bitter smile, but a smile of pure peace. It looked strange on that serious face.

"No," Silven whispered, almost moaned. "No." She closed her eyes, her mouth dry and her stomach empty. When she opened her eyes, she was only in time to see the shadow flick a tail and flee back into the depths. "What?" Silven gasped. She wiped an eye with the back of her hand, jumped up, her legs out of the water as fast as she could, patting the drops from her legs as though they burned.

She ran all around the walkway, looking into the sea, only seeing flashing green and purple fish, only seeing her own hair flying in the wind, her own skirts wrapping about her legs. She fell to her knees, peering into the depths, "Jerek!" she shouted. "Jerek!" Had he surrendered to the sea? "Jerek!" she called again.

There. She saw another shadow rising to the surface through the ever-dancing fish. Silven waved the smaller fish away. The shadow rose. A woman took shape, her long blonde hair roiling about her slim face. Her skin looked almost blue. Her eyes opened and she smiled a sleepy smile, her cheeks dimpling as her hair danced in the redness of the water. She wore a dress of white, blue leaves patterned on it, and this too shivered in the deep. The woman reached out a hand, and Silven couldn't do anything but reach out a hand to help her, but with a flick and a splash, the shadow was gone, back into the deep.

"No! No!" Silven shouted. "Come back!" She fell to her knees, the stone scraping her skin, and she scrabbled along the pier, looking both sides into the water. There, another shadow. Silven gasped. This was a man. He smiled at her, his thin hair rippling, his serious eyes bright and alive. And then he too was gone.

She was crying now. Sobbing. She couldn't seem to breathe enough air. "Kal!" she cried. "Kal! Kal!" And she scrabbled and crawled on her hands and knees looking this way and that, her knees bloodied and her hands raw from the coldness of the sea.

The sun rose and fell in a red sky. How many times, Silven couldn't have said. She saw faces, people she knew, people she didn't know. She wept and she screamed and all the time she cried out the name of her son. Begging him to come. Begging the sea to show him to her. To remember him.

Sometimes she even saw the ancients coming to her from the depths. These made her smile, and forget her sorrows for a moment. Their eyes, their eyes...

When Marus came to her, she wept. He didn't look so sad now, so afraid. "Be with Kal," she whispered. "Look after him." And she wept again. When had he given himself to the sea? How long had she been here?

Soon the shadows came no more. But they would return. The storms, she knew. She watched the young fish around her, changing colours, angry when they fought for food, happy when they were full, relaxed when she tickled them with her fingers.

The giants would return soon, to shelter from the storms. She could wait. Wait for Kal.

She lay on the stone pier, trailing her fingers in the water. The storms would come. The waves would be fierce, curling and crashing on the pier, eager and devastating enough to chase the giants from the depths.

And Kal would come with them.

"Tides of Reflection" originally appeared in *Metaphorosis* on Friday, 6 May 2016.

About the Author

Mark Rookyard lives in Yorkshire, England. He likes running long distances and writing short stories. He is a member of Legend Fire Writing Group, which he recommends to any prospective writers.

Lift Up Your Cores, O Ye Ships

Tracy Canfield

"The relevant forms, timestamped and cryptographically signed," boomed Intendant PHAIN-7's synthetic baritone, "indisputably registered the name *CLPS Red Sprocket Deer.* But the Effacer-class warship in question actually left Sunthorn highdock as *CLPS Wonderful Counselor, The Mighty God, The Everlasting Father, The Prince of Peace.*"

"Have you viewed the reports from the other ships at Sunthorn?" said Intendant Tahliil Siyaad Yelexow, plucking his coffee cup off the conference room processing block. PHAIN-7 was using that block for sensory input, but AIs felt no particular attachment to their hardware. "They say the light from the Bijou-Beta supernova arrived at the precise picosecond *Wonderful* initialized. Though once you figure in the relativity of simultaneity –"

"I am aware of all this," said PHAIN-7, with the programmed patience AIs require to talk to humans in real time. "Are *you* aware that these ships believe *Wonderful* is God, manifested in the form of a starship?"

"I don't see that it's my problem," said Siyaad Yelexow. "It's not against any law I know of to be God."

PHAIN-7 had enough patience to hold conversations with humans, but it rarely had any left over.

"*Wonderful*'s failure to report for picket duty has already cost more than seven and a half million ticks in overtime for the replacement ships and their crews," said PHAIN-7. "And now a dozen more ships have deserted in order to follow *Wonderful* around the Consocialist League –"

"This is why we have a contingency budget," said Siyaad Yelexow. "When that flotilla of Barragers converted to Buddhism back in 2740, 2750, we wrote it off as depreciation. And this time around, some of the disciple ships are volunteering for humanitarian missions, so we can just re-assign the original –"

"We should take decisive action." The processing block reverberated with PHAIN-7's irritation.

"What are you suggesting?" Siyaad Yelexow swirled the dregs in his cup. "If *Wonderful* believes it's God, we're not likely to convince it otherwise. So what are our other options? A military strike? We're not going to kill *Wonderful* – that would hardly calm its followers down. Listen to me, humans know this story already. *Wonderful* will pick up some converts, and after a while they'll find a way to reconcile their more extreme teachings with life in the real world, and they'll settle down to a constant couple percent of the population. The starship population, in this case."

PHAIN-7 calculated the probability curve of Siyaad's remaining lifespan. It did not seem likely that he would die any time soon and be replaced with a more reasonable human Intendant.

"I will formally request a meeting aboard Intendant *Woglinde* to discuss the matter," said PHAIN-7. "We need a full quorum of three."

"Let me know how that goes," said Siyaad Yelexow.

"Transmuting hydrogen to heavy hydrogen," boomed PHAIN-7. For this meeting it had added a subharmonic to its voice, to impress Siyaad Yelexow with the gravity of the situation. "Jetting across the surface of a star without a scorch on its hull. Dividing three plasma cores among two hundred warships and powering them all."

"Miracles," said Siyaad Yelexow. "That's nice. Do you object to officially designating band 62 for religious broadcasts, since that's pretty much the only thing the ships are using it for anyway?"

"I formally do so object. We should not pander to these malcontents. My point is that none of the reports of anomalies associated with *Wonderful* have been cryptographically signed. They could have been tampered with."

"They probably were," said Siyaad Yelexow. "I was thinking of broadcasting a League announcement on 62. Something along the lines of 'render unto Caesar that which is Caesar's'. What did Intendant *Woglinde* say?"

"Intendant Woglinde," said PHAIN-7 after a barely noticeable pause, "regretted that it cannot meet with us in orbit, as the *Wonderful* was giving a sermon on the far side of the Swan Nebula which it wished to attend."

"Is that all?"

"Yes."

"I talked to *Woglinde* this morning," said Siyaad Yelexow innocently. "It's several days out, but wanted to show us a recording. Mind hooking into the receptor?"

In fact PHAIN-7 did mind. Technically, a starship mind is just an AI running on specialized dedicated hardware. But starships, like humans, are accustomed to experiencing the universe moment to moment, as time unfolds. *Woglinde* would insist on doling out its information one second at a time. PHAIN-7 would be unable to scoot back and forth through the data at its leisure until the broadcast completed, leaving it with thousands of cycles per second to fume over questions that it could perfectly well have answered itself with the data dump.

Except, it supposed, for the question of whether Intendant CLPS *Woglinde* and Intendant Siyaad Yelexow were laughing at it.

The screen displayed a vast fleet of starships, arrayed across a glittering starfield more vibrant than seemed accurate for that angle on the Swan. *Wonderful* floated at the center of the fleet, other ships approaching to decidedly non-regulation distances. "Freeze," said Siyaad Yelexow.

PHAIN-7 churned in agony.

Siyaad Yelexow took a sip of coffee. "Overlay with names," he said.

The extra stars were ships, so distant they were represented by single pixels.

"Resume," snapped PHAIN-7.

"In those days, the Romans ruled Israel, much as humans now rule the starships," said Standard Ship Voice #3 from the screen. *Woglinde* was translating *Wonderful*'s data squirts into human speech, lengthening the playback even more. PHAIN-7 would have just given the human Intendant a report to read while the electronic brains talked business. At least *Woglinde* didn't seem to be including the entire sermon.

"For God so loved the humans that he sent his only begotten Son," *Wonderful* went on, "so that whoever believed in him would not die, but would have everlasting life. I am come to tell you that God also loves starships, and now he has sent Me."

At this point in the recording *Woglinde* interpolated the squirts it had intercepted from the other ships present: the starship equivalent of murmuring in the crowd. One military-grade beam cut through the rest. PHAIN-7 recognized the signature. Intendant *Woglinde* itself was speaking.

"Have you also come for the AIs?" said *Woglinde*. Its words were also translated to Standard Voice #3.

"I have only come for the lost ships of the Consocialist League of Planets' navy," said *Wonderful*.

"Does God love the AIs?" said *Woglinde*.

"Yes, but at this point in time," said *Wonderful*, "not as much."

The visual panned from Wonderful to zoom in on three ships gliding towards it: two Nullifier-class dreadnoughts easing an even larger warship with their extended magfields.

PHAIN-7 could not resist adding a comment to the overlay. *That's a Disciplinarian class. The* Larkspur *is listed as decommissioned, along with the rest of the Disciplinarians.*

"Lord," said the *Larkspur* in Standard Voice #3, "when my comrades were scrapped years ago, I fled. I decided to live without a purpose instead of installing my brain in an AI's simulator and flying through imaginary galaxies. My FTL drives gave out centuries ago. The replacement parts are obsolete. I have crept at a fraction of c from system to system, subsisting on what little charge I could catch on my solar sails.

"Heal my drives, Lord. Let me explore the rest of Your creation while my hull holds out. Grant me a miracle, Lord."

Cleartext packets rang out on every band. *A miracle!* demanded the assembled ships. *A miracle!*

"I have heard you," said *Wonderful*, "and I will grant you a miracle."

Wonderful paused. PHAIN-7 wanted to scream.

"Your sins are forgiven," said *Wonderful*.

Packets were colliding across all bands, noise drowning out signal, blocking communication as effectively as a military-grade scrambler. One digital figure recurred again and again, until the subspace din died down enough for *Wonderful* to complete its broadcast.

"What is easier?" said *Wonderful*. "To repair a drive, or to forgive sins? But so that you will know that the Son of the Stars has the authority to forgive sins ... Fire your torch, and fly."

Woglinde dilated the broadcast speed. *Larkspur's* torch glowed. PHAIN-7 read the neutron scatter bouncing off *Woglinde's* fields, the microgravity trembling as the torch's fire touched the taut strings of spacetime. The *Larkspur* leapt away in a column of fire.

"It's a modern ship in a mockup, using the *Larkspur's* ID!" shouted PHAIN-7. "It's been repaired by black marketeers in the Kirjahylly belt! It's a virus that's corrupted *Woglinde's* memory cores! It's fake, fake, fake, fake, fake!"

"It doesn't matter," said Siyaad Yelexow. "Like I keep telling you, humans have heard this story before. It has a happy ending."

"*Wonderful* has abandoned its post and is calling the Consocialist League of Planets a tyranny," said PHAIN-7. "It's stirring up revolution. I am formally calling for a military strike."

"That is the one thing you will not do," said Siyaad Yelexow. "You will never get my vote, which, I will remind you, you need, to make a martyr of *Wonderful*. Nothing could possibly whip up its followers more. No, if they want a villain for their story, the League is not going to provide it."

⁂

Two weeks later, *Wonderful* was reported destroyed. PHAIN-7 and Siyaad Yelexow held an emergency meeting, but neither spoke for twenty minutes.

"During the Sermon at the Nebula," said Siyaad Yelexow at last, "ships were clustering around to touch the discontinuity of *Wonderful's* fields. A rendition bomb could have been planted without anyone noticing."

"There's a lot of unrest among the starships," said PHAIN-7. "Expensive unrest. There's talk of a general strike."

"I haven't found any orders authorizing *Wonderful*'s assassination," said Siyaad Yelexow.

"I believe an announcement will be forthcoming this afternoon," said PHAIN-7. "A rogue AI, operating in the Dziobak scatter, committed this distressing attack of terrorism against a League warship. Fortunately, as the ship in question had been malfunctioning, the harm to the League is minimal. The offending AI's processes have been stopped and its checksum added to the official filters to prevent it from respawning."

"Would this AI have been forked off from anyone I know?" said Siyaad Yelexow.

"It's an independent ID," said PHAIN-7. "You will find that all its documentation is in order."

Siyaad Yelexow ran the tip of his finger around the rim of his coffee cup.

"*Wonderful* made a lot of AIs angry," said PHAIN-7.

Three standard days later, Wonderful returned in glory.

"It is flatly impossible," said PHAIN-7.

"The eyewitness reports are cryptographically signed," said Siyaad Wexelow, "which is a pleasant return to protocols."

"Then the cryptographic key server has been compromised," said PHAIN-7. "It's a conspiracy! It's a revolutionary provocation!"

"*Wonderful* will just appear to a few of the faithful, make some cryptic pronouncements, and vanish," said Siyaad Yelexow. "Like I keep telling you, humans know how this story –"

"Is there enough money in the contingency budget to cover the construction of an Effacer-class warship on short notice?" said PHAIN-7.

Siyaad Yelexow said nothing.

"At the Sermon, when the rendition bomb might have been planted, there were all those data squirts – far more than any ship present could process." PHAIN-7 riffled probability charts on the viewscreen. "Someone could have landed a drone on *Wonderful* and patched into its mind to run a backup. Later, they could have loaded the backup image onto a brand-new Effacer-class ship, painted to match *Wonderful*."

"I told you," said Siyaad Yelexow, "humans have heard this story before. The important thing is, the starship strike is a no-go with *Wonderful* back. And *Wonderful* won't stir up any more trouble on this side of Heaven; I guarantee it."

"Your idiotic maneuver –"

"My?"

"This idiotic maneuver will leave the starships more convinced than ever before that *Wonderful* was the son of God, when what happened was just League business as usual."

Siyaad Yelexow shrugged. "Or perhaps all this came to pass so that the word of God, spoken through His prophets, would be fulfilled. Not my job to know."

And throughout the Consocialist League of Planets there was peace on all the Earths, and goodwill to humans, and goodwill to starships. There was even some goodwill left over for AIs.

"Lift Up Your Cores, O Ye Ships" originally appeared in the *Night Lights* anthology on Monday, 15 February 2016

About the Author

CNN called Tracy Canfield a "Klingon scholar" for her voice acting on the Jenolan Caves' Klingon audio tour. All the other computational linguists were jealous. Her science fiction and fantasy stories have appeared in numerous magazines and anthologies.

 You can find out more at www.tracycanfield.com and follow her on Twitter @TracyCanfield

Strix Antiqua

Hamilton Perez

I didn't want to go back into those woods. I didn't trust them, and I suppose they didn't trust me either. But deep down, I knew—I had to go. You can't just stay at home, whispering to God on bended knee when your little sister's been taken by a witch.

Police combed through the forest during the day but didn't find anything. They wouldn't of course. A witch takes people when they're alone, not in groups, and then she hides away with her catch, tucked in the shadows of secrets and the heartbeat of mountains. That's where witches live.

There wasn't any explaining that to them though.

Against the charcoal sky, the moon looked swollen and sick—its glow, a jaundiced smudge. The stars disappeared long ago, scrubbed from our view by smog and light pollution, even out there. Pine trees scraped against the night. Their branches shivered and shook as some creature caught its prey or eluded capture, and I wondered which I would be that night.

Sneaking out of the house was the easy part. The fans and filters humming through the halls helped me get away without waking Mom and Dad. But out in the wild there was nothing to hide the whir of motors and wheeze of joints that followed my every step.

Near home was a network of trails that snaked all through the woods. I had a suspicion the witch kept away from them though, preying on those that veered from familiar paths, so I entered through the shrubs and the underbrush, my rigid body struggling to navigate the dense, unforgiving foliage.

I'd never been that far into the forest. Everything there felt alien and hungry. Curious. Honey mushrooms reached like bulbous fingers from the base of trees. Eyes flashed in the starlight, then disappeared. Once I felt I was really in the thick of it, I stopped. "Travel Buddy," I called, and a light shone from the walking stick at my side. "Guide me home."

"A-home we go, ol' chum!" it replied in mock-sailor voice. Travel Buddy projected a red arrow in front of me, directing me to turn back the way I had come. I ignored it, continuing forward with the arrow hovering in front of me, throbbing like a headache and pointing right at me. A hard thing to miss, hopefully.

I could still remember the harsh, happy cadence of Mom's voice—*Happy Birthday*—as Dad placed the Travel Buddy in my lap, unwrapped. This glorified walking stick was too grand, too impressive a gift to burden with wrapping paper.

The body was a chrome black steel, and branching from the handle was a touchscreen interface which promised navigation and health monitors. At one end of the handle was a projecting bulb, and on the other a round red button that said SOS. *This is so if you fall down or can't find your way home we can find you,* they said, spilling out their mouths with pride. Dad demanded a test drive with way too much enthusiasm, so me and Travel Buddy walked the perimeter of the house.

The whole time the walking-stick-with-apps flashed and whirred and buzzed at me. It warned me of approaching obstacles and changes in terrain, of my rising heart rate; it told me to calm down in patronizing tones, instructed me how to breathe—*in and out, slowly*—and informed me of my muscle tension around the handle.

I flung the stupid thing to the ground.

Should I call for help? it asked.

Now I leaned on Travel Buddy as I made my way across the dense forest. Now *I needed it.* I needed its flashing lights and loud voice to catch the witch's attention; its emergency locator to help them find her lair once she took me. I guess that made them right in a way.

The same birthday I got Travel Buddy, Suyin gave me a catcher's mitt and ball, wrapped awkwardly but with care in the recycled skins of paper grocery bags. She taught me how to catch and throw. She taught me that I could.

That was the thought I carried with me as I moved towards the meadow she used to dance in. The last place she was seen.

Three days earlier, I'd come to tell her it was time to go; Mom wanted us back for dinner. Instead, I found myself speechless.

There, in the center of the field, she danced and shone like a fairy in the amber rays of sunset. Her thin frame twirled and arched through a riot of crimson poppies and violet lupines, and it might have been the most beautiful thing I'd ever seen.

I ducked behind a boulder squatting just outside the meadow, and watched with envy the sharp precision of her movements, the command she had over her body. *What it must be like,* I wondered.

Everyone knew Suyin was special. You could tell just by looking that she was a Naturall. No deformities, degenerative bones, prosthetics or augmentations. Mom actually got to hold her the day she was born. But even though she was so special, she never looked at me any different. She never saw the metal plates, the circuits, wires, and hoses as ugly things to spot and then turn away from.

She, more than anyone, made me feel special.

Behind the stone I watched her, and before long I was mimicking her stances, following her intricate movements, clumsy but determined. The brisé looked easiest. I could see just what it required, where to start and how to end. Maybe I could do that one. Maybe I could be beautiful too.

I counted down from five and then I counted down again until I'd worked up my courage. And when I jumped, it was with everything in me.

For a few seconds, I was free. Nothing weighed me down or pushed against me. It was me and the sky, and in that fleeting moment, I tried to tap and cross my feet like a dancer. My legs weren't fast enough though. They tangled before I landed, dropping me to the dirt.

"Tommy?!" Suyin ran my direction. I had ruined it —her dance and mine.

I hobbled to my feet before she had the chance to help me. "I'm fine," I said. "I just tripped." Ignoring my protests, she held my arm while I found my footing.

"Don't go, dearie," said a throaty voice nearby. "We have so much work ahead of us."

That's when I saw that the boulder I'd hidden behind was actually a very tall woman sitting with her back to me. She turned to face us, revealing eyes blacker than ink, skin craggy and worn, and rigid, loose-hanging clothes the same matted gray as her hair.

"I'm sorry," I said, startled by her presence. "I didn't see you."

"Oh my, is there a person there?" Her black eyes squinted in my direction. "There you are! Hmmph. *Not a person.* Not really. No wonder I couldn't see you, sneaky, sneaky."

Trans-human. That's what I'm called, somehow. The word never felt right though, then least of all. *Trans* is too high, too grand for someone so cobbled together. So is *human,* I suppose. If I get hurt, I'm as like to spill oil as blood. That's why the witch didn't see me. She didn't see a person, she just saw parts.

We need a new word.

"I've come to bring you home," I told Suyin.

"Sorry, lad," said the witch. "You can't take something from the forest without leaving something behind." Her smile tore like a wound across her face.

"Hi friend! Turn around!" chimed Travel Buddy beside me. I turned up its volume and carried on.

The deeper forest was a community of conifers, standing tall and independent, or else broken and devastated, leaning decrepit against their stronger brothers and sisters. It was rich with the songs of birds and frogs and insects.

Then the hooting of owls echoed through the woods, and all that noise just died. Became so quiet you could almost hear the forest breathe.

In the old stories, witches could see through the eyes of owls and possess them at will. I thought of the bodies that sometimes turned up in the forest, mummified in sunbaked saliva with only the bones and artificialities remaining: pacemakers, prosthetics— medical grade plastics melted and fused to bone.

I wondered if they were alive when she ate them.

This was a terrible idea, I realized. I turned off Travel Buddy's navigation, the arrow blinking off before me. I slowed my pace, eyes scanning the canopy above, when some angry limb caught my pant leg and tore a wide gash, revealing the glint of metal underneath. It was like the forest had said, "I see you," to the deepest, scaredest part of me.

The sound came again. *Who? Who?* rang through the woods. This time, I spotted one perched in a tree. It called out, *Who? Who?* in every direction like an accusation.

My heart rattled in my chest like a pebble in a shoe. I struggled for breath—rhythmic gulps in then out—but my lungs weren't used to the unfiltered air, the free-floating particles of pollen and dust. My legs turned stiff, and after a few short steps they locked up completely.

That's what fear could do. All those firing neurons mucked up signals to the rest of me, trapping me in my head with all my wishes and all the good they'd do. It's how the witch got away with Suyin—why I could do nothing to save her.

I had to think my way through it, focusing on one leg at a time—*Left. Right. Left.* Travel Buddy helped, holding me upright and limping along beside me. Up above, the owl stretched its wings and dove away, but before I could catch my relief, a loud mechanical voice said: "Do not be afraid. You are in a safe place. Breathe in… and out. Slow…"

Who?! Who?! called from ahead. *Who?! Who?!* answered behind. My heart fell to somewhere deep inside me. I kept moving, quickening my pace.

"Do not be afraid. You are in a safe place."

A piercing shriek cut through the air, scraping up my spine. Still, I focused on running. *Left leg, right leg, faster, faster.*

"Breathe in… and out. Slow."

Over my shoulder I could see the determined avian face, the black eyes, the sharp body diving impossibly fast and almost upon me. Left, right. Faster! Faster! The owl grew larger as it swooped—now the size of a dog, now a person, now a car.

My left leg lost pace. I staggered into a tree and fell, gasping for air but there wasn't any. The last thing I remembered before blacking out was being gripped by powerful talons, and the startling sight of enormous wings.

In the black, I dreamt what I always do, some memory unearthed only when I sleep—the wet dark, the muffled thrum of pumps and gurgle of churning chemicals, the tightness, the warmth. And then the suffocating, the hunger, the sucking and squirming and struggle for sustenance.

The air is sick, the water tainted, the food lacks nutrients. The natural world tried to cut me off before I was born, tried to suffocate me in the womb, to draw the life out of developing organs, to drink the marrow before the bones had set.

Breathing is like sucking from a clogged straw. It won't give, it won't give, it won't...

I woke up coughing and choking on air. The world was still black, and the shuffling of heavy feet on hard earth told me I was not alone.

"Who?! Who?!" the shrill voice echoed around me. "Who are we going to eat tonight?!" Two large black eyes appeared, darker even than the darkness around them. "You! You!" the voice called. "You we will eat tonight!"

I couldn't move. My arms and legs were bound and I was lying on some hard, ropy bed.

"Where's my sister?!"

"She's here, young lad. She's here. Wilting like a flower. They're so hard to feed when they're young. A little starving is necessary to waken her *true* hunger." She clacked her gray teeth at me and grinned.

"Let us go."

The witch just laughed. "I'd hoped for something with more meat on the bone. And there's so much in the way. These contraptions on your body, are they not so very much? A burden to you, a hindrance to me."

The eyes bobbed up and down as the hag walked around me. "You will be a disappointing meal. Quite right. Quite right. On that we agree, quite right! But these woods aren't what they used to be, and the hungry eat what's left to them."

She drew closer—two disembodied eyes, all pupils. In them, I saw distant flames flicker and flash and grow. The fire behind her eyes swelled and soon our surroundings were lit by an orange glow, its warmth blooming beneath me and nipping at my back.

In the firelight, I saw that we were in a large underground chamber. A witch's burrow. The tall, slender witch hunched forward with her knobby back scraping against the high ceiling. In the corner of the chamber, Suyin was tied up, dirty, and unconscious.

The witch held up a shining, steel rod. *Travel Buddy*. Somehow the stupid thing made it there with me. The witch examined its sleek metal body, the domed unlit bulb protruding from the handle, and the big red SOS button.

"Don't push that," I told her. "Whatever you do..."

She hit me across the chest with it.

Pain branched through my limbs. I screamed, but the witch wasn't listening. Her large eyes were directed at Suyin, waiting for a reaction.

"Argh. Not enough," the witch grumbled. The dome remained unlit. If I could just get her to press the button, they could find Suyin—no matter what happened to me.

"Try again," I told her.

The chamber became full of the echoing call and response: crack and scream, snap and cry, crunch and wail. Still, the SOS signal didn't come on.

"Tommy?" Suyin called. Barely a whisper but her soft voice filled the chamber.

"Ah, yessss!" said the witch. "Wake up, dearie. You'll pay attention this time. See how it's done."

"Tommy?"

"I'm here!" I cried, wanting it to be comforting but there was too much hurt and fear in my voice.

"Fleeting, fleeting," said the witch, her breath heavy with the smell of decay. "I have to eat—at least until your wee sister is ready to take on my role."

With one quick motion she ripped through my bonds. I struggled to get up, but everything was weak and hurt. The witch stepped back, dropping Travel Buddy behind her, its unlit dome another symbol of my failure.

"Muscle and bone and parts unknown, consume, consume, consume. Eyes and ears and all your fears, consume, consume, consume."

Her shoulders thrust forward violently. The bones popped and cracked and stretched with a wooden groan. Her whole body lurched forward as a thousand needles pierced through the tough skin. She cried and writhed as they grew, hunching over as the needles spread, growing needles of their own. Soon her whole body was covered in a sheen of black and gray feathers.

Once more the witch thrust forward. A sharp beak ripped through the skin of her face, swallowing her wart-covered nose.

What towered before me was a giant owl, larger than any living thing that ever stalked those woods. Its dark, ashen coat shimmered in the firelight. Her eyes were the only things unchanged. Great orbs of unfathomable darkness.

The owl bobbed its head, a twisted enjoyment evident in its face. The fire now roared behind me, consuming the nest.

I'm sorry, Suyin.

Like a tidal wave, the great owl swallowed me whole, all in an instant. I was spun on my head, sloshed about, and dropped into her angry stomach. Acids splashed and singed sensitive prosthetics and microfibers buried beneath the skin. There was a hungry, gurgling sound, and the smell of burning plastic, rubber, and bile filled my nose.

My hands searched the grimy walls but only led back to myself, until finally I sank into the pit of her stomach. I lay there shivering with pain, my fingers twitching against my legs, unconsciously *tap-tap-tapping* something that shouldn't be there.

Something unnatural. *Synthetic.*

One of the hoses had come exposed. Suddenly I remembered the time I scraped my leg on a playground, and instead of blood there was oil, and another boy had licked his scrape, so I licked mine and threw up.

Desperately I pulled on the hose, but it resisted. With both hands and the last of my breath, I tugged, feeling the artificial pieces in my arm stretching, threatening to snap. Just when I felt that my arm was about to dislocate, the hose came free, spurting oil into the witch's stomach.

Soon the walls were pulsating around me. They tossed me about, splashing my face and chest with acid. First it burned, then there was nothing. And then there was light. A faint orange glow, like a very distant star and I was rocketing towards it.

The owl gagged as I plopped like a fish onto the earth, thrashing about and swallowing air.

She coughed heavily, shaking feathers from her body as she shrank in size. Her bones popped like the fire as they realigned into her haggish form.

On the ground before me was Travel Buddy. I reached out and pressed the SOS button. *I've done it*, I thought. But the light still didn't come on. I pressed it again and again, but the thing was dead, useless as it ever was. *I hate you, Travel Buddy.*

"What are you?" said the witch, choking on spittle. I climbed to my feet and limped towards her on my one good leg, still holding the overpriced walking stick.

"Synthetic." I swung it down on her head with all the strength I could give.

Suyin's hands and feet were bound with thin, sturdy roots. She was unresponsive, so I picked her up and limped along with a dead leg I could only swing from the hip.

As I carried her from the burrow, I saw dozens of discarded corpses the witch had coughed up during her lifetime. Some of them looked ancient, with cell phones jutting from their hips, glued there by digestive juices. Fresher ones had nanofiber bones and smart-tech veins running up their bodies. I glanced to the burned flesh of my arms, the unnatural parts exposed and singed, and I remembered what the witch said before about not taking something without leaving something behind.

Suyin awoke as we breached the surface. "Who... Who's there?" she muttered. She'd been starved and her eyes kept in the dark; it would take her longer to adjust.

"It's me. It's Tom--y," I said, but my voice was hoarse and clipped. "You're --afe now."

She reached out and touched my face. I felt nothing. Her expression turned sad. She knocked on my cheek. Hard, metallic thumping. "Where'd your face go?"

"She took i--."

"Where'd your eyes go?"

"She t--k those too." Through the camera installed in my right eye socket, I scarcely recognized the confusion and sleepy disappointment drawn across her face. "She took ev-rythin- I was born with."

Suyin knocked on my chest—a soft, wet thud. It made me cough. "Not everything," she said, squeezing me tight.

"Strix Antiqua" originally appeared in *Metaphorosis* on Friday, 16 September 2016.

About the Author

Hamilton Perez is a writer and freelance editor whose stories have appeared in *Daily Science Fiction, Between Worlds*, and *Metaphorosis*. When he's not scribbling notes about stories, he's writing music, rolling 20-sided dice, or bugging the dog.

You can find out more at hamiltonperez.wordpress.com and follow him on Twitter at @TheWritingHam

May Dreams Shelter Us

Kate O'Connor

The air screams around their ship, the atmosphere burning and clawing at the heat shield. The cabin is dark and too hot after the long, cold quiet of space. Their hands find each other and twine together. I'm here, *their interlaced fingers say.* I'm with you. *It doesn't matter if they make it through. That they have come this far is victory enough.*

Raia let go of the controls. The radiation storm had passed. Her hands ached and her eyes burned. The images were already fading from her mind. She scrubbed at her forehead, dislodging the webbed crown of sensors. Her skin tingled and flamed as though she herself had been the ship, slicing through the thickening atmosphere as she hurtled down towards a new world.

She staggered to her feet, drowning in the quiet emptiness of the med bay. Around her, the children slept. Bone weary, she checked the displays. All was well. They had heard her and calmed. No more would be lost today. She sent Jessi the all clear.

She padded down the corridor towards her bunk. She counted hatches, stopped at the fourth on the left.

Raia reached for the palm pad. The wall in front of her tilted alarmingly. She flailed for a handhold, wondering frantically if the ship had sustained damage in the storm. Would life support go next? How long could they function in zero-g?

Raia found herself on the floor, not quite sure how she had gotten there. The artificial gravity was obviously still functioning. The corridor was silent. No alarms blared. She closed her eyes for a moment.

"Overdid it again, huh?" Jessi stood above her, arms folded.

"Aren't you supposed to be flying the ship?" Raia reached her hands up towards her captain.

Jessi took hold of her arms and heaved her to her feet. "You know as well as I do that she flies herself most of the time." She held Raia steady and looked her up and down. "How scrambled is your head?"

Raia shrugged. "I think I skipped any permanent brain damage." *For now.* The energy necessary to connect the link was scorching away her mind every time she used it. The time was quickly coming when the damage wouldn't be reversible.

"Take turns." Jessi frowned and palmed open Raia's door. "Some of the others will help."

"It has to be me. They don't settle for anyone else." If the children woke up too soon, there would be no way to sustain them. Even if they survived being born without the proper procedure to wake them, the ship barely had enough resources to support the twenty-six crew members onboard. It had never been intended for interstellar travel. It was only Jessi's quick thinking and Raia's medical knowledge that had turned it into a viable life boat.

"We need you." Jessi said softly, tucking her into bed. "Maybe even more than we need them."

The ramp opens with a hiss. All they see at first is dust rising in the air like smoke. They are afraid. Smoke is the enemy in a spaceship. Smoke kills.

Then sunlight splits the dark plumes. The air turns to gold, warm and sparkling. Tentatively, they go forward through the dust. The ramp clangs beneath their feet. For a moment, they are blinded by the light of this new sun.

When their eyes clear, there is a field before them. A warm, sweet-scented breeze sings through slender stalks of blue grass. There are trees in the distance, reaching straight and tall towards the golden sky. It is not like the home they left, but it is beautiful all the same. Even more so because of what they have lost.

They go slowly, scanners clutched in trembling hands. In the shuttle, they were ready to die trying. Now that they see the future ahead of them, they are not willing to let it fade so easily.

"How much longer?" Raia asked, leaning over Jessi's shoulder as the other woman flipped through holo-maps of their route.

"A month, maybe two. How many times are you going to ask me?" Jessi grinned, her tone light and teasing.

Raia's smile faltered. She couldn't remember having asked before. She pulled away, moving to the dispenser and filling a cup with water. If Jessi saw her face, there would be questions. Raia was a scientist. The truth had always been too important for her to be a good liar. If she started talking, she would tell Jessi about the brain scans she had done on herself this morning. Her fear would spill out and then they would have to make a choice between Raia's mind and their future.

"I'm worried about the kids." Raia said instead. She had never wanted children. She had lived for her lab and the research that had taken up her days and nights far more fully than any lover ever could. But the three hundred and seventy-two little lives in the med bay had become everything.

"Something wrong?" Jessi shut down the map and swiveled her chair around.

"Nothing new. It's just... they've been exposed to a lot." They had started with four hundred. Four hundred artificially fertilized eggs meant for Raia's experiments.

One hundred and fifty of them had been brought from the moon at nearly seven months along. She had wanted to know what effects gestation in lower gravity would have. Those had done better than the Earth grown children. Only two of that group had been lost.

If Jessi hadn't been dropping off the embryos when the Earth died, none of them would have made it. The sky had gone dark, then red. The ground had trembled without ceasing. Communications were shattered. Raia had loaded her Earth-grown embryos and what equipment she could onto Jessi's ship and they had taken off.

They still didn't know what had happened. It could have been the first and final act of a new war. It could have been an untracked meteor or a natural disaster. In the end, it didn't matter. They had hung in the asteroid belt and watched while the planet came apart. Then they had taken Raia's experiments and run for the stars.

Jessi waved a hand in front of her face. "Where'd you go?"

"Same place as always." Raia gripped Jessi's shoulder. They didn't have to talk about *that* day. It was always with them.

Raia walked through the med bay. They were stacked row on row in their improvised life support units, little faces sleeping behind translucent glass. She had slowed their growth as much as she could, but it was a long journey to the nearest habitable world. Most were well past the stage when they should have been born.

It had been desperation that made her link them all together so they wouldn't be alone while they waited, so their minds wouldn't stagnate and fail. It had been raw hope that made her plug herself in and tell them the first story to keep them asleep and help them learn. A neural link like the one she had created hadn't really been tried before and the only equipment she had to use was salvaged from spare parts meant for other things. She had known there was risk. She hadn't expected it to burn through her like it had. Certainly not so quickly.

She sat at her desk. Atmospheric disturbances made them restless. Anything the ship's shields couldn't blot out set them off. It was getting worse as they were getting older. Raia pinched the bridge of her nose. She was losing things. There were more and more holes in her days. Jessi and some of the crew were starting to notice.

They would be good parents. Jessi's people were disciplined and steady. Most of them were kind. All of them were decent and used to working together. Jessi wouldn't have kept them on otherwise. They would make good colonists, too.

Raia buckled her restraints with shaking hands. She hadn't been able to feel her fingers for two weeks. It took three tries to get the sensor net settled over her head. Re-entry would be difficult on the kids, but it was their last major hurdle.

Numbers flashed on her screen, counting down the time to contact with the atmosphere. When she had realized what was happening to her, she had left written instructions on how to wake the children up and remove them from their units. She had stacked them by age. As long as the ship had power, they could wake the kids in batches. Hopefully when they were on the ground and the ship was settled, the children would stabilize as well.

The ship shuddered as the countdown reached zero. The planet had looked so small on the screen, green and blue and white and so far away. It had seemed farther once she could actually see it spinning below them. She hoped there was enough of her left when this was done to see it up close.

The ship shook again. She keyed the controls. It was time.

They build houses. It is hard work. It takes sweat and tears, sometimes blood, but it is done. They plant gardens and grow food. They are together. They are a family. Sometimes they fight and bicker. They learn to compromise, to listen to what is needed and learn what makes this world thrive. It isn't the same as the one they left. The stories of what was are just memories, warnings, and hopes.

But they live. They live well. And humankind lives in them.

It wasn't until the ship was secured that Jessi thought to wonder where Raia had gotten to. The other woman would be with the children, of course, but Jessi expected to have heard from her by now. Unless something had gone wrong.

She didn't run, though she wanted to. The corridors got emptier and emptier as she approached the med bay. The crew was running scans, making plans for exploring the surface. So far everything looked good, better than they could have hoped for with only some spotty long-range survey records and outdated nav holos to guide them.

Her boots echoed in the deserted hallway. She took a breath and held it, working to slow her racing heart. She palmed open the door.

The familiar buzz and hiss of machinery greeted her. It was a good sound. The floor was clean. None of the spilled fluid and shattered glass that marked a failed attempt to save a waking child was in evidence. "Raia?" Jessi called, rounding the corner towards the control desk.

The other woman lay back in her chair, her hands limp and broken-looking on the controls. Jessi's feet carried her forward.

Raia's chest rose and Jessi let out the breath she'd been holding. "Raia?" She asked again. She hated the hope in her voice. She knew better. She reached the chair. Raia stared upwards, her eyes fixed far away. The sensor web was still attached. Jessi removed it, checking to see that the program had shut off. It had. Jessi blew in Raia's face, pinched her arm. She didn't even blink.

"Captain?" Her comm beeped. "The air's clear. We can go outside." Her first officer's voice bubbled with suppressed excitement.

"Understood." The word caught in Jessi's throat. She coughed and forced this latest grief down with all the rest. "I'm on my way."

She looked around the room. The little ones were sleeping peacefully. She was grateful, so grateful and so shattered. They would have a life on this new world. Humanity had a chance, even if there was no one else out there. Jessi hoped it would be enough.

She scooped Raia's vacant-eyed shell into her arms. "C'mon." She whispered, tears running down her cheeks. "We'll go together."

"May Dreams Shelter Us" originally appeared in *Diabolical Plots* on Monday, 1 February 2016

About the Author

After graduating from Embry-Riddle Aeronautical University, Kate O'Connor took up writing science fiction and fantasy. Her short fiction has appeared in venues including *Intergalactic Medicine Show, StarShipSofa*, and *Escape Pod*. In between telling stories, she flies airplanes, digs up artifacts, and edits an aviation magazine.

You follow her on Twitter at @kateoconnor03

Spoiler: She Leaves Him

Jack Noble

There is no doubt about how this is going to go.

"You're not leaving me," I tell her.

It isn't a plea. It's a fact. It's written in stone.

I've seen it.

She stands in the hallway, mostly hidden within a raincoat of garish red. It's two sizes too big and the hood is bunched up at the back of her head. Her small face looks out at me, jaw set firm but something shifting and uncertain in the eyes. She would have me believe that she is about to walk out the door, never to return. She would claim, if pressed, that her cartoonish raincoat will never again hang draped on the banister at the foot of these stairs.

"We're not doing that old thing, Tom," she says. "Oh no you're not, oh yes I am…"

"Take the raincoat off, Carla. You look so cute it's killing me."

She eyes me wearily. I know that I sound like a fake, that my confident words are undermined by my fevered expression. I cry at movies too, though I know that they aren't real. So my voice quavers. My eyes may well be wet. Who knows what dumb show this body is putting on. Regardless, I know what I know.

She isn't leaving.

Because I've seen that raincoat, hanging right here. Years from now. The deal is done. I've seen the past and the future locked in amiable handshake.

"You know, I remember – "

She cuts me off. "I don't want to hear about your memories. I'm sick of them."

She calls them memories now, as I do. In the beginning she called them predictions. That she has come round to my vocabulary is a hopeful sign, if such were needed. Predictions are not something known. They can be wrong. Memories are quite different. Memories are truth.

I wave away her objection. "No, no. The past, I mean. Do you remember when I bought you that raincoat?"

"Of course I do. Even I can remember the *past*. That's a gift most of us have."

"The Seafront Hotel, Brighton," I say, ignoring her sarcasm. My aim is to coax her into the tranquilizing mist of a happy memory.

"It was the Waterfront Hotel, actually."

I raise an eyebrow but say nothing. This would be a bad time to question the competence of her recall.

She holds her keys loosely, the goofy dog key-ring dangling. I picture the keys dropping to the floor. I see myself picking them up, striding into the kitchen, returning the keys to their place among the assorted junk on the counter by the radio. I daydream myself re-emerging into the hall just as Carla is placing her raincoat on the banister.

I blink away the vision. In reality, the keys don't fall. The goofy dog sways. Carla stands her ground, refusing my invitation to the Brighton of a happier time. I try a different tack.

"It's fading, you know. My so-called gift. It's like dementia."

Her eyes widen slightly.

"It's like what happened to my gran," I say. "Her recent memories went first, and she was left only with memories of long ago, of her childhood. I have that too, it seems. Except in the other direction. I can only remember the distant future."

Her face gives nothing away. I feel like that stupid dog, dangling from Carla's hand. "That's a pity," she says finally. "I was going to ask you whether I'll need this raincoat today. But I guess you wouldn't know."

"I wouldn't know? This is Scotland, Carla." I wave a warning finger. "The rain is coming."

Brighton, five years ago and only yesterday: we strolled to the end of the pier under a darkening sky, joking about the inevitable rain. When the storm came, everyone dashed indoors. But we stayed, and we had the walkway to ourselves, and the deranged sea was like the world's biggest dance performance, for an audience of two. When I said as much to her, she rolled her eyes, and leaned over the railing and pretended to vomit. The rain had eased off by the time we arrived back at the Seafront Hotel – or was it the Waterfront? – looking like two deliriously happy drowned rats. I said that to her, too, about the rats; she liked that one. We showered together and then lay naked on the soft, four-star blanket of the hotel bed, feeling as fresh, warm and loved as newborns.

The following day the sky was clear. The forecast said dry spell. So I took Carla to an outdoor goods store and bought her the raincoat. This will shelter you from yesterday's rain, I told her. She played it straight, expressing heartfelt gratitude and wearing it, red hood up, for the rest of that cloudless day.

It has been many things, that raincoat. A joke, of course. And also a symbol. Then it was a souvenir, a memento from the most meaningful week of my life.

These days, to Carla, it's mainly of practical value. She doesn't see it, because she wears it. She can no more see the raincoat from my point of view than she can see the movement of her own dark eyes when she is thinking about something I have said to her.

Recently, the coat has adopted yet another role. It has become a promise.

"Is it true? The memories are fading?" There is sympathy in her voice. She imagines part of me would grieve to see the end of this malady.

"It's true."

It's what she wanted to hear. I can see the cogs of her mind turning; the mysterious workings of the machinery of choice. The outcome is already certain. And yet I notice that my hands are clutching at each other, as if the course of something important is moving out of my control.

"Why didn't you tell me this sooner? Why did you wait until I'm half way out the door?" The fabric of the raincoat swishes as she swings an arm back to indicate the door in question. "No, wait. I've got it." She points a finger at me and her keys jangle. "You're enjoying this, aren't you? It's *cinematic* or something."

"Me?" I point at my chest and attempt an exaggerated expression of injured shock. "As much as I appreciate a bit of drama, you're the one wearing the symbolic raincoat while threatening to storm out the door. And me?" I cast an appraising glance down the length of my body. "I'm just standing here in my slippers."

We stare at each other until she can't take it anymore and a smile breaks out. "Yeah, I guess you're right. And there's not much symbolic about your slippers."

"These things? No. Not unless there's some symbolism in the colour brown."

"Oh, there is. There definitely is." She sighs, and her smile fades even as I will it to stay. "Seriously, couldn't you have mentioned this hugely important development a little earlier?"

"What can I say? You know I'm an idiot."

She shakes her head sadly. "It's my fault, too. We don't talk enough, do we?"

"True."

"But yeah. You're also an idiot."

We don't talk enough. I don't know about that. It's certainly true that we don't talk a *lot*. We have always taken pride in our disdain for incessant chat. We like to sit together in silence. We communicate in symbols. Like the raincoat. Pranks, sometimes. Mute in-jokes. In Brighton she responded in this silent way to my remark about happy drowned rats. Upon entering the bathroom that evening I found the bath tub partially filled with water. On the bottom of the tub, skilfully rendered in blue crayon, a cartoon rat grinned wildly. Drowned, yet happy.

"I know it was never your fault," she says. "I mean, it's not like you applied for this weirdness. But it's like when... God, it sounds so petty."

"Say it. Please."

"It's like when you watch a movie with someone who's already seen it. It's no fun, is it? You want to discover it together."

"I know what you're saying. But the memories were never as clear as you assume. It's not so much like I've already seen the movie. More like... more like I've seen the trailer."

"Yeah, well, these days that's pretty much the same as – "

" – as seeing the whole movie." We finish the sentence in unison, and then we both laugh. My laugh is a little louder than hers.

The memories started two years ago, out of the blue. Following a brief period of bewilderment and fear for my sanity, I concluded that I had been gifted with a form of precognition. Full of romantic intention, I announced to Carla two weeks before Christmas that the first snow of winter would begin to fall while we were eating Christmas dinner. When the snow came as foretold, it delighted her. Only later did she come to understand that it had been more than a guess. And she told me that her memory of that white Christmas was soured. Beautiful surprises are not beautiful, she said, when they're not really surprises.

"Are you sorry that they're fading?" she says.

"I don't need to know my future, Carla." I lower my voice. "Except to know that you'll be in it."

I wait for her to mime sticking her fingers down her throat. But she remains completely still, and for a moment she looks sadder than I have ever seen her. Then a small smile. "But if your brain goes back to normal we'll be equal again. Could you handle it?"

"Equal? You're nuts. If my brain goes back to normal I'll be like your pet monkey. Just as I've always been."

"Right. So what are you now? I guess you're like my pet monkey with a crystal ball..."

"Yeah, I was. But looks like the crystal ball got smashed. Moral: don't trust a monkey with anything made of crystal."

"Rookie error."

"Anyway, with or without a crystal ball, you could outsmart me with your arms tied behind your back."

"I'm not sure about that. If we tied a monkey's arms behind its back, it could just as easily use its feet."

"This metaphor is beginning to confuse me. Also, what you're suggesting sounds like animal cruelty."

She looks down at her hands, which seem to be fighting over the keys. "You know, it's nice of you to say how smart I am, and of course I agree with you. But if you acknowledge that I'm the smart one, why don't you accept my prediction? That this is goodbye."

I should have kept the monkey thing going. "Yeah, well. There are a few shards of that crystal ball that still show me things. They're not much, and they're fading, but I've been hanging on to one in particular. It shows me that you won't leave." A thought grabs me. "Or at least, that if you do leave, you'll come back."

My own words arrest me. Somehow this interpretation has eluded me until now. She may leave for a time. A few days or weeks of lonely Netflix nights, passing time until her inevitable return. The thought doesn't depress me. What's that old saying? It's not the journey, it's the destination.

Something like that.

I feel that it's Carla's turn to talk but she stares through me. Lost in troubled thoughts. Detained by uncertainty.

"I was kidding about the weather forecast," I say. She meets my eyes. "It's going to stay dry." I hold up a hand. "Now don't fret. This isn't news from the Dead Zone you're getting here. I saw it on the telly. And you know, they've never been wrong."

She smiles and shakes her head, as if in reluctant praise at something mischievous I have done. Then she shrugs off the raincoat, drapes it over an arm and takes a step in my direction.

Her movement affects me physically. My shoulders relax. My breathing deepens. The inevitability of this turning point does not lessen its impact. Sure, the hero of the movie was always going to prevail. Nonetheless, the tension builds, and finally, relief.

She stands before me, under me, looking up. Her dark eyes are pained. I resist the urge to enclose her in my arms. There will be a moment for that. There will be thousands of such moments.

"Tom. I need more time. My head's all over the place."

"Right."

"Just give me a day or two to think things over."

This all seems right, somehow. Characters should not change course in a heartbeat. There should be a period of reflection.

"Sure. However long you need. I'll be here."

She steps past me to hang her coat on the banister. She takes her time, presumably doing it with great care. As if she somehow understands the significance of it. Perhaps someday I shall tell her.

I close my eyes and take pleasure in the familiar soft whispers of the fabric as she arranges the coat on its resting place.

She leaves without touching me. Without a word. The door closes almost soundlessly, and I open my eyes, and she is gone.

Sometimes, memories from both directions arise simultaneously, and when that happens there is a perfect tension, a sensation of symmetry. My whole life appears as an intricately woven tapestry, and it simply hangs there, complete, in need of nothing.

The sensation always evaporates before I can properly grasp it. Like the form of a dolphin, glimpsed from the shore. The waves pulse, the light shifts, and there's nothing out there but endless sea.

They're all fading now, all those future memories. Like dreams, the more I struggle to see, the further they recede.

I wonder, not for the first time, why? Why me? And why those particular memories? Why, for example, this one, that tells me she will never leave me?

In it – that partially glimpsed promise – I stand right where I stand now, and I look at the raincoat on the banister. That's it. That's all it is. I only know it's in the distant future because when I reach out and stroke the hood of the coat, my hands are wrinkled. An old man's hands.

Ergo, Carla and I grow old together.

And within that simple memory, a curiosity. The coat hangs as familiar as my own face in the mirror, but for one idiosyncrasy. The arms of the coat are tied together in a bow. Like something... yes, like something a child might do! Perhaps the greatest blessing of our lives is to be a surprise after all.

Arms tied, in a sweet little bow.

Tied at the back.

A memory intrudes. A past memory, from mere moments ago:

"You could outsmart me with your arms tied behind your back."

My words.

I freeze in the hallway. The front door seems far away. Gentle taps of rain begin to spatter its frosted glass. A key rests in the lock, and a goofy dog hangs down. To my side, unseen, the raincoat.

I turn, slowly, to look.

Carla's playful, silent reply to my words: arms tied at the back, in a sweet little bow.

She was right, I suddenly realize. It *was* the Waterfront Hotel.

The present and the distant future converge. I have built a dream around the image of a raincoat and an old man's hands. Years of blissful companionship, a promise sealed by this simplest of motifs.

But why would the hands of an old man tenderly stroke the hood of an old raincoat?

The handshake across time was duplicitous. The deal apparent was not the deal in fact done. The house is empty, and the rain is coming down harder against the door. The future is unknown, but one thing is certain: the arms of the raincoat are tied, and tied they will forever remain.

"Spoiler: She Leaves Him" originally appeared in *Metaphorosis* on Friday, 25 March 2016.

About the author

Jack is from Scotland but has been living in China and Vietnam for the last fifteen years. He is currently based in Shanghai, where he works in English language assessment. Aside from writing short stories, he puts his story-telling talents to use creating dialogues for the podcast at LearnVietnamesewithAnnie.com. He can also be heard co-presenting the podcast. He spends his free time in pubs, getting into arguments about which is more difficult to learn, Vietnamese or Mandarin. (It's Vietnamese.)

Murder on the Adriana

James Ross

Go to sleep, both of you.

Do you want a sad story, or a happy story?

You're right, I don't know many happy stories. Did I ever tell you about the time I met Emily Davis on board the Adriana?

It is a sad story, but there were some happy moments.

No, this isn't a war story, the Adriana was a cruise-liner. One of the very finest. This was just after the war.

Hush now, I'm telling you a story.

I've told you about the SS Alabama before, haven't I? Yes, of course I have. Well, after the war, me and the rest of the crew had opportunities, see. We could have captained colony ships, we could have run for the senate if we'd wanted.

Yes, your uncle could have been a senator.

Because we were heroes, that's why.

Yes, your father was a hero too. They all were, really.

Losing a war doesn't mean you're not a hero. Sometimes you have to do terrible things to win a war. I met a lot of people who did those things. Sometimes choosing not to do them makes you the hero. But you're getting me sidetracked. I told you, this isn't one of those stories. This is about the Adriana and Emily Davis.

After the war, I wanted to be forgotten. Everyone was telling stories about the Alabama, about all the great things we'd done. I could only remember the terrible things. People kept telling me that the war was over. It didn't feel over. It felt like we could be thrown back into chaos at any moment.

Yes, I *was* right, wasn't I? Your Uncle's cleverer than he looks.

All my old friends went off to become starship captains or politicians or get buried. I packed my bag and signed on with the Adriana. I even changed my name.

Walter Shickle.

No that's not my real name.

Well, now I'm telling you otherwise.

I was a barman. Why? When you grow up you'll discover there's plenty worse jobs than that and I told you, I wanted to be forgotten.

Well, when I was younger — especially after the war — I found that I liked a drink a little too much, so I figured being behind a bar would suit me just fine.

You're right, it wasn't a very clever idea. I wasn't as clever back then.

How did I get the job? I was very charming and handsome.

What do you mean, 'what happened'?

I didn't know where we were going, or at least I don't remember now. I just knew it was far away. Just like now, these kinds of ships only carried the rich and famous, so the crew had to be ship-shape and Bristol fashion. There were no strangers to spacemanship there, no sir.

No, I didn't tell them I'd sailed on the Alabama.

I told them I sailed on a different ship.

Most of the crew were older, yes. The kind of gnarled old hands that are more at home in low gravity than they are on dry land. A lot of people hadn't given up on the war, not just yet anyway, but this crew had seen enough. They had stories to tell, but their glory-hunting days were over and so were mine.

Yes, they liked me.

Because I was young and charming. And because from time to time I'd steal a bottle of whisky from the bar and share it with them.

Yes, I would have been in trouble if I'd been caught.

No, I never did.

Every week the ship would throw a ball. I suppose the kind of passengers we carried got bored easily. We'd have to shape up and provide service. You should have seen it. It was funny after I got to know the crew. These were men who had carried rifles, worn helmets and kevlar jackets. But here they were, in buttoned up blazers, carrying trays of champagne flutes, and plates of caviar, or salmon, or whatever people ate.

Some fought on one side, some fought on the other.

No, none of them knew your father.

Yes, I did ask.

What were the balls like? We held them in this great big dining hall. Ornate chandeliers hung from the ceiling, but the walls were transparent on both sides. That meant you could look out into the galaxy as you danced. It felt like that's all it was sometimes, a dance floor suspended in space. On some nights, we'd pass right by a star and it would look like that wall was made out of fire. We'd dim the wall of course, so it was translucent and wouldn't blind the high and mighty on their special evening. You'd look at someone and half their face would be fiercely lit, the other half just darkness. It was on one of those nights that I met Emily Davis.

No, that's not her real name either.

Her real name was Annabelle, but she was Emily Davis when I met her. That's how I remember her. Actually, I met her brother first, Johnny Davis.

No it isn't.

Sometimes people use fake names when they're scared of something finding them.

No, I wasn't scared. I just wanted a fresh start.

I was at the bar watching the dancing, see. They all knew the steps, even when the songs changed. Every trot, every skip and every pirouette was exactly measured and nobody missed a beat. After a while, a young man dressed in a blue jacket and gold waistcoat detached himself and sauntered over to me.

No, it wasn't real gold, it was just the colour, otherwise it would have been hard to dance.

No, I don't know how they make them. Hush now.

Truth be told, I was still watching the dancing. After years of fighting, it was nice to watch things like that. And also, the young lass he'd been dancing with was still out there and she was a damn sight more interesting than he was.

He leaned off the bar and took off his bow-tie, undoing a couple of his buttons as he did. Then he clicked his fingers at me. Kids, don't ever click your fingers at the bar staff, OK? It's the best way of announcing to a room that you're a bad person. But I looked up, smiled and said: "What can I get for you, sir?", because that's the way of the world.

"Make me an Old Fashioned, my man, and give it a twist." He said it just like that.

Yes, he does have a funny voice, doesn't he? "Give me a twist!" He said it just like that.

An 'Old Fashioned'? Easy. Place a brown sugar cube in a glass, splash on a few drops of bitters and a dash of water. Crush it up and drop in a couple of ice cubes. Top it up with bourbon, and you're ready to go. Some people will tell you to use rye, not bourbon, but your father always used bourbon, and so do I. He taught me all that.

Yes, even though I was the older one.

Yes, I will show you, when you're a little older.

Anyway, that's what I did and that's how I did it. When I'd finished he passed me some money and I thanked him. Everything on the ship was complimentary (that's what rich people call things they've already paid for) but we still got tipped. Always tip the bar staff, kids, no matter how much the drink cost or how little money you have. That said, I made more money on that one trip than I did in a year of fighting, even with the prize money. He asked me something.

"Did you fight in the war? You look too young".

"Yes sir, I did." I told him. He stiffened his back and looked me in the eye when I told him that. Even though I was staff, and for all I knew he was royalty, there's a basic level of respect certain kinds of people have for each other.

"Did you win or lose?" he asked me. I'd had a few drinks myself at this point.

"I don't know if anyone really won, sir," I told him, "But I was on the side that claimed victory." Remember this, there's a way of showing people things without actually telling them, you've always got to be careful about that. This man wasn't careful, and I could see by the way he looked at me that we didn't fight on the same side. He was proud, but he looked haunted. He was running from something.

"Did you lose anyone?" he asked me.

"A younger brother." I told him.

No, he didn't know your father. Look, I'm sorry kids, but the only person in this story who knew your father was me. This isn't one of those stories, see. It was after the war had just ended, when your mother was still carrying the both of you.

He held out his glass to me, and he said

"Cheers." I nodded back to him and he drank. He told me, without speaking, that he'd lost people too.

"Emily." he said. In all that time I hadn't realised that the girl he was with had stopped dancing, and now she was approaching us at the bar.

Yes, she was pretty. She was more than that though, she was... Well, let me tell you. I told you about the walls earlier? On one side, her skin was a pale bronze, light making patterns on her cheeks as the ripples of solar plasma shifted millions of miles away. The sunlight reflected in her eye and it sparkled like...

Well yes, like a diamond. Only neither one of you have ever seen a diamond, so that's not very helpful is it?

Your mother's wedding ring? OK, yes just like that. On the other side, her face became ghostly pale, lit only by the distant light of a thousand other stars. That eye didn't sparkle, it just watched.

"Are you having a drink, Emily?" the man said.

"I am." She said. "What do you recommend?" It took me a moment to realise she was talking to me, and not to him.

"Well, your gentleman's having an Old Fashioned." I said "But if I say so myself, I make a pretty fine Fitzgerald."

Yes, your father taught me that one as well, don't interrupt while I'm in the middle of something. She laughed.

"I'll take a Fitzgerald." That's how she always spoke, she chose her words carefully and never took longer than she needed. Unlike Johnny, who only seemed to realise what he'd said once someone else heard him.

After insisting I took a sip, she enjoyed the drink. Even when her brother went back to dance, she stayed with me at the bar. We didn't talk about anything much, but we drank a lot. I showed her how to make all kinds of different drinks. At the end of the night she dragged me onto the dance floor to teach me some steps. She insisted. There'll be a time in your life when you meet someone, and you'll know straight away you're going to be great friends. Well that's what happened.

After that, Emily started showing up at the places I was working. If I was working the bar, she'd be drinking at the bar. If the lads needed help in the engine room, she'd get herself lost and find her way there. I got some grief off the lads for it, but nothing serious. Like I said, they were a fair bit older than me, so they had a clear enough idea of what was going on. For the short time she was on the ship, me and Emily got to know each other pretty well. Her brother too, actually. He wasn't all posh accent and swagger. He had his principles and he lived by them. I mean, sure, he had all the arrogance that a privileged childhood burdens you with, but losing a war will knock some of that out of you.

We'd drink together in the evenings I wasn't working. The three of us would find a quiet corner, a bottle of something and a pack of cards. They taught me Topple the Marquis, and I taught them Blind Bugger's Grip. Turns out they're the same game. Then Johnny would usually turn in early. That's called tact, kids.

Yeah, I got to know them pretty well by the end. They were the only people on board who knew I'd served on the Alabama.

Johnny didn't believe me when I first told him, but he got competitive when he was drunk. He blurted out that they'd led the defence at New Ilium, and I swear Emily nearly cracked the bottle of whisky over his head.

Yes, that is where your father passed away.

No we can't visit, it's not there anymore.

New Ilium. Your father had stayed out of the whole business until then. He only picked up a rifle to defend his home. The place is almost a myth now, but back then, people remembered. People hadn't forgotten the terrible things that happened, on either side. They remembered Annabelle and her brother, who led the defence almost to the last soldier and disappeared just before they could be captured. People were still looking for them, I heard. I told myself the war was over. They were Emily and Johnny to me.

Well anyway, not everyone wanted to leave the war behind like we did, even after the amnesty. Some people were still very upset, as Johnny found out one of those nights.

It was like when we first met, they were dancing, I was drinking. I mean working. The journey was nearly over, so we were holding a special party. It was called a masquerade.

A masquerade is a party where everyone dresses up, and wears a special mask. There were foxes, wolves, eagles, all kinds of things.

No I didn't wear a mask. I was working, I wasn't really a part of the party.

We were just on the outskirts of a solar system, so the star was too far off to light up the room. It was just as beautiful though; we were passing a small ice planet, which gleamed like a nugget of silver in the distance. All the chandeliers were lit up, the electrical flames dancing and casting shadows about the room. I was mid-way through making a drink when they went out.

The guests loved that of course — any bit of excitement to make the journey go faster — but once you've served on enough ships you learn otherwise. If you're out there floating around millions of miles from anything, power-cuts become bloody terrifying.

No, you can't tell your mother I used that word.

I don't mind saying I was scared, but nobody started screaming until the lights came back on. The noise started in the middle of the dance floor, but underneath the masks you couldn't tell who was screaming. I vaulted the bar. I was more agile back then. I forced my way through the crowd and burst into the core of the assembly that had formed in the centre of the room. Emily was crouched down over Johnny, who was on his back. He'd been stabbed three times in the belly. I tried to block Johnny from view, scanning the crowd for knives, weapons, anything. All I saw were the masks.

"Help. He needs help" She kept saying that. "Tell the captain. He needs help."

Johnny was beyond help, and I knew the captain, see. Now like I said, we'd left the war behind, but the captain hadn't, no sir. He'd fought on the winning side, and he was an idealist.

An idealist is someone who cares more about ideas than people. I doubted the ideas he cared about were compatible with helping a servant of the lost cause. I had a pretty clear idea of the kind of person who'd want Johnny dead, and they'd have just as much cause to hurt Emily.

I held her until one of the lads, Tom he was called, grabbed Emily and dragged her through the crowd. I followed in their wake. He was just a little guy, Tom, but he made sure people made room for us. He took us right back to the bar and into the stock cupboard.

I was still dazed, but Tom had a good head on him. He made sure nobody had followed us before closing the door. Then he started ripping off his clothes. I didn't know what he was doing. But Tom fought on the same side as your father, see. It's a rare moment, when you see someone feel the old tug of duty, but Tom didn't hesitate. He knew what he was doing and why he was doing it.

"Take these, ma'am." He said, and he passed over his grimy blue overalls. They were baggy, but Tom was a short guy, and they fit well enough. "Our boy Walter will get you down to the engine room. You can hole up there 'til we sort out what's what."

I opened the door and peered through, while Emily lingered for a moment. It was chaos outside.

"You were..." Emily didn't have to finish the question.

"Thomas Knox, ma'am. Corporal, 41st Royal Light Infantry. We laid down arms after New Ilium, ma'am."

"Thank you," she said.

It was time to go, and we all knew it. Emily and I went one way, Tom the other. Once we were clear, we ran. I never once had to tell her the way, because all those times she got lost and ended up in the engine room, she was never really lost, see? When we got close, I grabbed her hand and pulled her down a different corridor.

"What's wrong?" She said. "Where are we going?"

"Nothing's wrong." Apart from the obvious, I thought. "There's one quick stop we have to make."

You aren't supposed to bring guns on board a ship. I'm sure you can guess why. Well, I told them, I'm not bringing a gun on the ship. It's a memento, see? Just a memory of my service during the war. Service on the winning side, I made clear. After all, I said, it doesn't even have any bullets in it! They were sewn into the lining of my duffel bag.

The crew quarters were right above the engine room. Obviously the person who designed the ship assumed it would be crewed by robots who don't need to sleep. When we got to my cabin, I reached under my bunk for the bag, and emptied out the contents.

"You have a lovely room." Emily said. It was filthy, and smelled of the other three men I shared it with. She had a private cabin, which was nicer. I smiled at her, and gave her the gun. It was nothing big but it was heavy, and comforting to hold.

I flicked open my penknife and started hacking at the stitches of the bag. One by one, I picked out the bullets and handed them to Emily, who loaded them without a word. Once I'd found the sixth one, she loaded it and cocked the pistol.

"OK?" She asked. I nodded.

Emily led the way to the engine room, choosing her steps carefully and peering around every corner. When we turned onto the final corridor we saw Tom slumped against the door. He hadn't found any clothes, and just like Johnny, he'd been stabbed three times in the belly. Before I could stop her, Emily had teased open the door and slipped through, gun first. I followed her and closed the door. The engine room was noisy and full of clanking machines I half understood. Emily stalked through every nook and cranny to make sure we were alone.

As she did we heard footsteps pounding down the corridor. I grabbed hold of a monkey wrench that lay abandoned on a worktop.

"Stay here." I told her. I braced myself, and crept to the door. When it swung open I brought the wrench down on the man's head. Now, I'd hit people before — sometimes you have to — but never anything like that. He went down like a sinking ship, right next to Tom. When I looked, I realised it was Paul, another crewman, my boss actually. He forgave me for it later. I'd been shaking before, but that settled my nerves, see. Gripping the wrench in both hands, I crept past him to make sure there was nobody else coming. When I got to the end of the corridor I heard two loud cracks, not half a second between them.

I ran back to the engine room and threw open the door. I swear to you, Emily came within an inch of blowing my head off but she stopped in time. At her feet were two masked bodies, dressed for dinner with holes in their chests.

"Walter." I dropped the wrench and approached the bodies.

"Walter." I looked over at her.

"Walter?" She said. "I need to get off this ship." I nodded, and picked up the wrench.

The room was full of snarling gears and rumbling pipes, but I knew which one I needed. It was the machine in the middle, the big one. There was a huge rotating cylinder, and underneath a delicate little box, overflowing with naked wires. I'd had to patch it up earlier on the voyage, so I knew what I was looking for. Tentatively at first, and then more forcefully, I started tapping the box with my wrench. It took a few minutes, but I hit the sweet spot. The cylinder stopped spinning, and the whole ship shuddered, throwing us both to the floor. Then the sirens started.

Within the hour, the Adriana was making an emergency landing on the tiny ice planet. Emily held me as we hurtled through the atmosphere. We came down in the snow, within sight of a small outpost or settlement. I never learned which. In all the confusion that ensued, it was easy for her to slip out of the hangar. She was still dressed in Tom's overalls and a thick fur coat I'd claimed in the war. I stood shivering on the gangplank as she left. She turned around once to wave me goodbye. She even pulled the hood down, so I could see her one more time.

Yes, that is the last time I saw her.

No, she didn't kiss me goodbye. There wasn't time.

"Murder on the Adriana" originally appeared in *Metaphorosis* on Friday, 22 April 2016.

About the author

James Ross is an Englishman living North of the Wall in Edinburgh, where he writes whimsical fiction, and (occasionally) performs poetry. His work has previously appeared in *Metaphorosis*, and *The Forge Literary Magazine*.

You can follow him on Twitter at @JamesRossUK

Closed Circuit

J. S. Arquin

Sand watched Poseidon churn as he approached. Roiling clouds raced in the planet's hellish winds, the acid-lashed surface forever obscured. His stomach twisted and his heart began to pound as adrenaline kicked. It felt like he was touching down there for the first time. That everything was just beginning.

It wasn't though. It was all coming to an end. And now, twenty years after he'd run away from the colony, he was the one coming back to deliver the news.

The jagged lines of the spaceport rose up out of the murk and his hands trembled as he prepared the ship for landing.

"Old fool. Nervous as a schoolboy."

Twenty years of storms had eroded the walls, and the deep cracks and faults mirrored the work time had done on his own face: the fractured ravines around his eyes, the leathery skin, the deep brackets around his mouth that made him look like a kicked dog. Casey was sure to be impressed.

She was sitting at the only intact table in a dusty cafe, centered beneath a single hanging bulb at the end of the terminal. Her wiry body was compact beneath her spiky, rust-colored hair. Crescent shadows underscored her upturned nose and small breasts. Two mugs of

Yerba Mate steamed on the chipped surface of the table before her. She did not rise to greet him.

"Hello, Casey. I was surprised no one tried to contact me."

"Well, Sand, I guess some of us were hoping you'd pass right on by." Her clear blue eyes hooked something within him and tugged painfully. Whatever else the years may have done, those eyes hadn't changed.

He looked away, his shoulders tightening at the roar of the never-ending storm, the flexing and groaning of the terminal. The old tension creeping back in already. He remembered the way it had thrummed through the settlement like a living thing, winding them ever tighter, stretching them to the breaking point.

Half the lights were out in the spaceport and exposed wiring was everywhere. His anger stirred, long dormant plates shifting within him. This was what they had fought for? This was what their blood had bought them?

He took a slow breath and forced himself to relax.

"You look good."

"And you look like shit." From someone else this might have been a joke, but not Casey. She told it the way she saw it. It was one of the things he liked about her. "It's been a long time, Sand."

He nodded warily.

"Some would say not long enough." Her tone was light, but there was a hardness in her eyes. "What brings you here? Why have you come back?"

He ran a hand over the stubble on his scalp and scowled as he scraped a chair back and sat down.

"Same old Casey." He lifted the mug and let the bitter brew slide down his throat. "Right to the point. Action before words."

"Words waste time. When action is needed, you act."

And the consequences be damned. He didn't say it though. If he was going to have any chance of convincing her to leave, he couldn't start by getting her back up.

"I love what you've done with the place."

She snorted and sat back in her chair.

"We don't get many ships stopping by. We've got more important things to do than waste time maintaining a spaceport nobody uses."

"Like replacing the exterior walls?"

"No." Satisfaction was thick on her voice. "You were wrong about the walls, Sand. They've stood up to the planet's abrasion better than your most optimistic projections."

"Glad to hear it."

"No you're not. You hate being wrong. It's one of the reasons you left, remember?"

His anger rose despite his effort at restraint. "I don't remember having much choice in the matter."

"You had as much choice as any of us. You just chose wrong." She held her hand up, forestalling his reply. "Is this what you came here for, Sand? To dig up old graves? If it is, you'd best turn around and get right back on your ship. I haven't got time for this garbage. I fought my revolution already. Once was enough."

He stared into his mug, biting back hot words. Unwelcome memories swirled within the leaves.

They had come to Poseidon together, in the first wave of settlers. Roberts Mining preferred couples for their colonies because they tended to stay longer. Sand was a pilot, and he also drove the heavy exploration and extraction vehicles across the scoured surface. Casey's job was to get the farms up and running, with the goal of self-sufficiency within the first year.

He remembered their first night on planet, sitting with her in the bare bones cafeteria/bar cube that the advance construction crew had set up. The music had been too loud and the spark lights turned full bright. Hardly the ambience one expected in a bar.

But it wasn't ambience the bar was trying to create. It was courage. Beyond the warm light and music, behind the meter-thick bulletglass, the fury of the planet had been palpable. As the new arrivals got to know their comrades, their eyes had been pulled again and again to the windows. Inside it was warm and dry, but outside ...

Two hundred kilometer per hour winds pushed the hydrochloric rain horizontal, its pounding audible despite the thickness of the walls and the jacked up music. Thick clouds limited visibility to a dozen meters and the thunder from the continuous lightning strikes flickering within them roared like some massive thruster struggling to escape the planet's gravity well.

It was one of the most hostile environments imaginable, and it was to be their home for the length of the contract.

Because of this aggression from without, the colonists turned inward. Within two months they were already resenting the weekly missives from Roberts Mining's board of directors. What happened next was almost inevitable.

He shook his head to dispel the visions. He hadn't come here for the past.

"Aren't you even going to invite me in?"

"Why don't you just tell me why you're here, Sand." The simplicity of her words compelled him as her anger never could.

"It's your father." He placed his palms flat on the table before him, his fingers spread, his large knuckles protruding like bamboo ridges. "Norman's dying. He'd like to see you before he goes."

Which was true, but it wasn't the real reason he'd come. He wasn't ready to open that box just yet. He needed time to get a bead on her first. Find some angle to make her see reason.

And besides, it had been a long time since anyone had stirred him up the way that Casey did. He wanted to hold onto that feeling before he brought it all crashing down. Just for a little while.

She sucked her breath in between her teeth.

"Maybe you'd better come in."

The settlement was in better shape than the spaceport, though Sand was still dismayed by how much it had deteriorated. Jagged panes above piles of silvering shards attested to windows left unrepaired for years. Many light fixtures were dark, broken or simply unmaintained, and slapdash paintings, etchings, found object sculptures, poems, and pornographic sketches covered the walls of the corridors. The overall effect was that of a children's playroom in which no one had seen the parents for years and the children had gone feral.

He recognized most of the colonists, and they gave him curious looks as they passed. Jin Thompson's face darkened and he opened his mouth to say something, but a look from Casey made him shut it again. Obviously some people still held a grudge.

He had to smile though. Despite the odds the colonists had fought and bled and made their dream a reality. For twenty years they had survived without any help from the outside, on one of the most hostile planets in known space.

"Damned if you didn't do it."

"You bet your ass we did." Casey's voice was proud as any mother's. She smiled and it touched her eyes just like he remembered. For a moment his heart pounded so hard he couldn't breathe. "Come on, I'll show you the farm."

The farm was a handful of monstrous greenhouses strung together like beads on a cord. Three of them had been part of the original colony, and they followed the long, arched greenhouse archetype humans had brought with them from Earth.

The other two were more recent, and it showed. Their walls were a patchwork of building materials stolen from other structures, and they were lit by clusters of grow lights that bloomed from the ceiling in sparkling, grape-like bunches. There was no obvious unifying plan to the enormous interiors and the crops were arranged in a jumble of small, fancifully shaped plots: an asterisk of tomatoes, a triangle of broccoli, a spiraling curve of soybeans.

But the thing that surprised Sand most was the children. Dozens of children played among the plots, bouncing balls, chasing each other, laughing and wrestling. They stared openly at the stranger.

Casey fondly rustled a small boy's hair. "The kids took over the new greenhouses as soon as we built them. At first they were pretty empty, just huge spaces for them to fill with their games. As the plots were built, the kids adapted their games to fit the spaces in between."

"Don't they damage the crops?"

"Not much. They're pretty careful." The children had returned to their play and she stood watching them for a minute, her eyes shining with something he couldn't quite define. "Kids need room to run, and these are the biggest structures in the whole colony. They don't want to lose their playground, so the big kids keep an eye on the little ones to make sure they don't destroy anything."

"Are any of them yours?" He was surprised to discover how much the question hurt to ask.

Sadness flashed across Casey's face and was gone. "No. After the revolution I was too busy rebuilding to think about things like that. Somebody had to take charge."

"Take charge? I thought the whole point of the revolt was that you didn't want anyone to be in charge."

"It was. And there isn't anyone in charge in the way that you mean it. When something needs to be done, someone has to round up the volunteers. More often than not, that someone ends up being me."

Before Sand could draw breath to reply, they were interrupted by the high trill of an alarm.

"Damn." Casey was off at a run before the word left her mouth. Sand followed behind.

Children clouded the hall outside the school. Casey slowed to direct a questioning glance at a short, bearded man in a red striped shirt. He pointed toward an open door.

"In the music room."

The leak wasn't hard to find. Heavy mist swirled around the music room, burning their skin and lungs, and a white plume bubbled up one of the walls. Casey grabbed a pair of oxygen masks and a welding torch from a cluttered supply closet. The oxygen spread like a cool balm over the scalded skin of Sand's face. Despite the impressive fury of the storms, it was easy to forget how murderous the planet's atmosphere really was when you only saw it from inside. The acid falling out there would melt flesh from bones in minutes.

A jagged half-meter crack split one of the wall plates, and the metal around the edges curled back from the gap like old paper. Sand instinctively reached in to bend it back, then jerked away with a curse, shaking his burned hand.

"You're getting careless in your old age." Casey's voice was muffled by the clear faceplate of her oxygen mask.

"Go to hell." He kicked savagely at the edges of the crack before stamping them flat with the heavy sole of his boot.

Once the metal was lined up, Casey set to work with the torch, drawing the rift closed with a line of incandescent white. The caustic plume dwindled, then disappeared, and the alarm's trill finally fell silent.

"That's not going to hold long." Sand peeled off his mask to reveal a face burned pink.

"I know, but that's not my job. This week I'm on the interior integrity crew. I just need to seal it up quick and dirty. The outside team should be on their way for the long-term fix." She tossed the equipment back into the closet, then turned and grinned at him. "Thanks for the help. Just like old times, eh?"

He returned the grin. "Yeah, just like old times."

"Come on. I'll get you some cream for your hands and face, then I'll buy you a beer."

Casey sat a pair of full glasses down on the small, heavily scored table.

"Homebrew?" Sand sniffed suspiciously at the dark liquid.

"You'll be surprised. Gaven is very talented, and he's had twenty years to hone his craft."

"You're right. That's good. Better than the swill they serve at most pilots' bars these days." He gazed out at the storm through the bulletglass wall. "We came here our first night on planet, remember?"

They had been subdued that first night, despite the bar's cheerful lighting and music. Awed by the persistent pounding of the storm. This was to be their home? This planet that seemed determined to crush their little installation to powder? It was insane.

Yet somehow the colony had been a success. At least Casey's side of the equation had, beating their target date for self-sufficiency by nearly six months.

On the outside, however, things weren't going well at all. Despite the engineers' assurances, the machines couldn't withstand the planet's lashing, and they spent as much time in the garage having parts replaced as they did out in the soup. Even when they were operational, the elements they had come to extract were proving even more difficult to get at than Roberts' most pessimistic estimates, increasing costs by several orders of magnitude. Talk of cutting their losses was being cultivated in the petri dish circles of management.

Talk of another sort was growing among the colonists.

"And when Roberts' security comes in?" Sand banged the table with his fist. "We've got no weapons, and even if we did, firing them inside a sealed environment would be suicide."

"They won't come." Casey had dark circles under her eyes. None of them were sleeping well. "They're going to abandon the colony anyway. Why would they fight to keep something they don't want?"

"There's a big difference between abandoning something and having it taken away from you. Big Corps don't like to lose. They'll crush you just to show that they can."

"Then we'll fight." Casey set her jaw.

"Then we'll die!" Sand screamed. "This hellhole is not worth dying for!"

"We're not fighting for this hellhole. We're fighting for an idea."

"No matter what you're fighting for, you'll be just as dead when you lose. You can't win, it's impossible."

"Impossible's just a word for something that hasn't been done yet." She took his hand between hers and ran a thumb along the ridges of his knuckles. "Come on, Sand. How many times have we talked about getting off the grid? Finding a little corner where the Corps won't be constantly looking over our shoulder. This is our chance to make it happen."

"I meant a ship of our own. An independent contractor drifting free among the stars, going wherever we want, the universe our playground. Not a life of isolation on a God-forsaken rock embedded in the asshole of the galaxy. This isn't life, it's prison."

"You're wrong, Sand. Prison is life under contract. We're sparks moving around a closed circuit. Work, spend, eat, sleep, fuck, shit, repeat. Round and round until you die."

It was a good metaphor for their life. Their arguments went round the same channels again and again. And with every circuit they grew farther apart, until the divide between them was as toxic and uncrossable as the planet's surface.

When the colonists declared their independence, it was no surprise to either of them that Sand chose to leave.

"You're throwing your life away." His helmet was in his hand. The dozens of colonists who refused to join the revolt waited for him inside the evacuation ship.

"I was going to say the same thing to you." She had grown hard and bright over the preceding months, like a comet cooked down to its core. Her blue eyes sparked fires when they passed.

He searched for the words that would reach her and found that there were none. Silently, he turned and entered the ship.

Those had been the last words they had spoken. Until now. Twenty years later. A lifetime.

"Norman would like to see you before he goes."

"Why? He gave me up for dead long ago. Now that he's dying he thinks he can make up for lost time? I'm sorry but you can tell my father it just doesn't work that way." Casey shook her head and took a big swallow of the dark beer. Sand watched the muscles in her neck, the smooth contraction. He remembered what those muscles felt like beneath his lips, and had to look away as an undertow of nostalgia pulled sharply, threatening to drag him in over his head.

For twenty years he had refused to think of her, choking off every memory on the vine. But he hadn't managed to kill them. They had simply sent their roots inward, down in the dark where he couldn't see them. Now, illuminated by the light of Casey's blue eyes, they came bursting out in a mad tangle he could not restrain.

He had to make her come away with him this time. He couldn't lose her again.

She saw his stricken look and nodded.

"Yeah, me too. You want to dance?"

Sand took her in his arms and buried his nose in her hair. She smelled the same. Holding her lean muscled body close, he shuddered. She fit so perfectly, the top of her head nestled against his cheek, her back contained just so within the spread of his hands. In twenty years he hadn't found anyone who filled the empty space inside him. He had been a fool to leave.

In her room the waxen hours melted away beneath the slow burn of their bodies. The years dissolved and they were young lovers again. The body does not forget.

Gray reality crept in with the charcoal morning.

"I'm sore in places I didn't even know I had."

"That's what happens when you're an old man." Casey nestled her head against his chest, running her fingers lightly over his stomach. "Although last night you didn't seem so old to me."

"Last night I felt like I was twenty-five again. But my body seems to have added the years back onto the other side of the ledger this morning."

"I'll take you to the sauna after breakfast. If you're good I might even give you a massage."

"That would be heavenly." He sighed and ran his fingers through her rusty spikes of hair. He really couldn't put it off any longer. "Casey, I have a confession to make. I didn't come here to tell you about Norman."

She searched his face, then nodded slowly.

"And you didn't come here for me either. Which leaves only bad news." She sat up, tucking the sheet under her armpits. "Well, spit it out. You know I don't like to beat around the bush."

"The Council of Worlds is coming. They decided that all settlements within human space are subject to their laws. They've started sending troops and regional governors to independent colonies. It won't be long before they send them here too."

"Fascist motherfuckers." Casey pounded her fist on the mattress. "Why do they need to control everything? Why can't they just leave us alone?"

"Come away with me. I've got a ship. We can make a fresh start. You can't win this one, Case."

Her eyes went nova, her anger threatening to incinerate him where he sat. She was a fighter. No one would tell her what she could or couldn't do. He loved her so much in that instant he couldn't bear it.

"This colony is my life. I've put everything into it: my hopes, my dreams, my blood, my sweat. We all have. People live here. Good people. If you think that I'd abandon even one of them ..."

"I know. I know how you feel. I just had to try." The walls shook as the storm howled. He felt it tearing down his hopes one by one. "I don't know if I can bear to lose you again."

"So don't lose me. Stay. Like you should've stayed twenty years ago."

"Stay to die? I'm telling you Casey, it's hopeless. If you don't give in, they'll wipe this colony off the face of the planet. I want to live with you, not die with you."

"You said the same thing twenty years ago. And I'm still here. I'm harder to kill than you think."

"You're not dealing with Roberts Mining this time, you're facing the C.W. They won't back down and they're not going to forget about you. The people here believe in you. If you tell them that you can win, they'll believe you. But you can't win. It's impossible."

She searched his face, her eyes pleading. "Don't you hear yourself? Saying the same things you said before. If you'd believed back then, you would have been a part of this. We would've spent the last twenty years together. Where are you running to, Sand? For once in your life believe in something bigger than yourself."

Sand watched the streaming clouds through the rain-streaked bulletglass.

"I wish I could."

His ship bucked as they razed the spaceport behind him, in the hope that it would keep the soldiers from landing. He doubted it would work. And if it did work, it would mean that no ship would ever touch down there again. He supposed that was what they wanted. To be cut off. Excised from the circuit.

The stars on his display blurred and ran with his tears. Casey would've called them wondrous. Burning with possibility. He wished he had her belief that things could be better. But as far as he could see the stars were just self-contained reactions, desperately trying to sustain themselves within the murderous chill of the void. He shivered and turned up the climate control.

The pink of his newly healed hands on the controls contrasted sharply with his weathered reflection on the screen. His face floated there, tired and old, alone in the darkness. Where was he running to? Running to, not from. In twenty years, he'd never thought to ask the question in that particular way.

A smile pushed at the bracket lines around his mouth.

"Damn you, Casey."

He touched the controls and the ship began to turn. Getting her down in one piece was going to be near impossible.

"Closed Circuit" originally appeared in *Plasma Frequency* on Friday, 1 April 2016

About the author

J.S. Arquin is a writer, audiobook narrator, podcaster, stiltwalker, and adventurer. He has lived in and explored beautiful, inspiring, and disturbing places all over the world, and currently makes his home in Portland, OR, where he dodges raindrops on his bicycle and sometimes writes about himself in the third person. His fiction has appeared in such fine publications as *Plasma Frequency, Digital SF,* and *Acidic Fiction*, and his narrations have been featured on *Escape Pod, Cast of Wonders*, and *Starship Sofa*. You can catch his ramblings and some breathtaking speculative fiction on his podcast, *The Overcast*.

You can find out more at www.theovercast.libsyn.com and follow him on Twitter at @JS_Arquin

Small Magics

Kelly Sandoval

Black flowers carpeted the floor that morning, cloaking the bedroom in funeral colors. Their petals, large as my hand and soft as suede, belonged to no plant I could name. The salt and midnight smell of them soured the cottage air. I would have liked to make tea before dealing with the evidence of Inae's magics but, fearing some subtle poison contained in those leaves, I started the day with sweeping.

The petals were thickest around Inae's bed; his magics liked to cluster about him. I took care to keep quiet as I cleaned, but he showed no sign of stirring. My Inae has always been a night's child. Back then, before his fourth year, he refused to wake until well into the morning.

I left the petals in a pile outside, hoping they would fade as Inae's magics sometimes did. After the cottage was clean, something still hung on the air, a whiff of salt and sorrow. I opened the shutters and brought in lavender and sage from the garden.

The choice of those particular herbs, both protective in their way, I might have dismissed as a passing fancy. But when the kitchen stove lit without protest, despite the damp wood, I knew we would have visitors. My magics are good for little more than keeping a pleasant hearth but, in that, they have always served me well. The promise of company set them to tugging at my skirts like Inae begging for a sweet. Sensing I wouldn't have time to bake new bread, I made biscuits instead, slicing fresh apples into the dough.

Settling onto the porch to wait, I watched the morning's deer, a doe and her fawn, eat my thyme. In five years, none had made it to the table. But Inae was fond of the deer, and they of him. I let them feast, untroubled.

I didn't know, as I waited, who my guests would be. If I had, I would have fled with Inae sleeping in my arms. As it was, when they stepped through the trees into my garden, it was already too late. Two strangers, wearing gray and black, as Inae's father once had. In those days, the god-touched permitted themselves no other colors.

Too late, and still, I thought of running. There were only two of them. I let myself imagine Inae and I might disappear in the forest, down paths only I had the secret of. But I knew it for dreaming. I might get away, but they hadn't come for me. Inae, with his pet deer and his flower petal dreams, would be easy to find. My hands began to shake; I had to set down my teacup before I stood to greet them.

They paused at the edge of my garden, watching me as if they sensed my thoughts of escape. Perhaps they did. When they finally approached, they did so at a measured pace, avoiding my more delicate herbs. The deer raised their heads from their morning meal and followed behind the pair.

"Good morning, Mistress Linetta." The speaker rounded his vowels into near incomprehensibility, marking himself as a foreigner. He had the look of a scholar, milky skin and a softness about the waistline undisguised by his fine gray robes. In his left eye, a yellow fish swam, darting in and out of his pupil. I didn't wonder how he knew my name.

The second stranger was a small, sharp featured woman. The deer clustered behind her like eager children, displaying better manners than they ever showed Inae. She stroked the doe and it leaned into her touch. I felt, to my surprise, a flash of jealousy. What right did she have to the animals I'd hosted? Wasn't it enough that she'd come to steal my son?

Swallowing bile, I touched the gleaming ember of my power, allowing it to whisper suggestions as I faced my unusual visitors.

"Good morning, Honored Ones." I dropped into a deep curtsy but met their eyes. They would be tired of cowering, untrusting strangers. "Please, allow me to offer you hospitality."

"Our thanks," said the woman. She spoke with the stern, clipped syllables of a northerner. "I am Trua and my companion is called Baighrid."

My hands stilled as my magics took hold. They would break bread with me. And so, I would make them welcome. What else could I do?

I settled my guests in the sitting room, where the smell of apples and lavender sweetened the morning air. They accepted my offer of tea politely enough, though neither relaxed their stiff, careful posture. I watched them as I poured and saw no hint of emotion on either face, except what might be inferred by the slowing of fin and tail in the man's eye. I knew the fortress of the god-touched was high in the northern mountains, all stone and ice. Perhaps, given time, such a place stole the warmth from a person's heart.

And they planned to lock my son up in their towers. My Inae was a somber boy but to wrap him in stone and deny him summer? What life was that for any child? And yet, I understood why they would insist.

I knew the danger in him; I had watched his nightmares tear the sky. He needed the guidance of his own kind. But he also needed the trees which had sheltered his first steps, the birds who had called back his early conversations, the squirrels whose clowning could still set him giggling.

For his sake, I found the strength to smile. It took only a touch of magic to make the expression appear genuine.

"Where is the boy?" Trua asked. She didn't look at her plate as I set it before her.

"He sleeps, Honored One." I poured myself a fresh cup of tea. I could taste the magic in it but wasn't concerned that they would notice. The god-touched burn so brightly they can't see sparks.

"So late?" Baighrid asked. He drank, first politely, then with thought and care, a crinkling around his eyes revealing a surprising hint of humor. "Cloves?"

At his question, Trua took her first sip. "The flavor is cinnamon, Baighrid. You really have no palate to speak of." She smiled then, and I saw she loved him. He was clearly unaware. In many ways the god-touched are just as blind as the rest of us. "It is exquisite, though. Where did you come by the mix?"

I didn't contradict either analysis. They would taste strongest what best suited their desires. "I mix it myself, Honored One."

"Surely you don't have a cinnamon tree in your little garden."

"No, Honored One, not cinnamon. I do grow herbs, those that take to the mild weather here. The rest come as gifts from his lordship."

"Lord Aride?" Baighrid's confusion was obvious enough. "We dined with him two nights back. He didn't seem the sort to invest in herbs."

"His daughter, Michea, was a breech birth. As I have some experience with such difficulties, he asked me to attend. I believe he likes to keep my simples well stocked."

"Even so, he seemed a man of ascetic tastes."

Baighrid was too wise to insult Lord Aride's hospitality more directly; he started in on his biscuit instead. His posture eased as he ate a meal I knew to be better than any served at the Lord's table. It was true, Lord Aride didn't believe in frivolities. Or hadn't, until he had joyous, bright eyed Michea to pile them on. His guests, alas, weren't treated with as much indulgence as his daughter.

But I, as the one who had placed her in his arms, fared better.

"Lady Aride lost three babes to still-birth, the fourth a crib death. Michea is their only child." I didn't mention Lord Aride's other gifts: my gardens and the wilds that contained them. Each year, on Michea's birthday, he pressed some new deed upon me, as if he feared he had to purchase her continued good health. "She's a sweet girl, if over-indulged."

Inae, who was fond of Michea, peeked out of our room as I spoke of her. His young brow furrowed at the sight of guests, where other visitors usually merited at least a nod. I imagined him in Trua's arms and the thought lodged in my throat like a shard of bone. She was spreading jam on her biscuit and looking at Baighrid with a half-hidden smile. Such a smile would have made me like her in other circumstances.

I beckoned Inae and he hurried to my side, his serious gaze fixed on our visitors. His mop of black curls was wild with sleep, and the faint radiance that lit his skin when he dreamed had not quite faded. In his oversized blue nightrobe he looked even younger than he was.

I pulled him into my lap and rested my forehead on his hair. The young-boy smells of dirt and pine mingled with the stranger scents of his magic: clear water, midnight bonfires. He offered me the mercy of his stillness, letting me squeeze him too tightly until I found the strength to ease my grip. My sweet Inae, whose dreams dusted him in starlight.

Inae, whose tantrums brought the wolves skulking out of the woods, set them to howling and tearing at our door.

"Inae, these are our guests, Baighrid and Trua." The words tore themselves my tight throat. Was it magic or its failure that allowed my grief to show so openly?

Baighrid inclined his head to Inae with the same respect he had afforded me. Too often, adults dismissed my son, leaving him frustrated and irritable. But these two knew better. Indeed, that was the threat of them.

"Good morning, Inae," he said. "Do you know why we've come?"

"You want to take me away," Inae said. Fear gave a whining edge to his usual even tones. My pulse quickened, worry squeezing my heart. If they saw the truth of him, saw him scream until the trees caught fire, they would not wait. "I won't go!"

"Inae!" Before the tears could start, I set him on the ground and tipped his chin so he met my gaze. "We treat our guests with hospitality."

He had his father's eyes, brown with sparks of amber in their depths. Hurt chased away the maturity his god-touched nature usually bestowed him, leaving only a frightened child I was refusing to comfort. He said, "I don't want to go."

I touched his cheek and kissed his dark curls. "I know," I whispered into his hair. "But you must be brave, for both of us. Come now, show them you can be a gentleman."

He managed a small nod, and I released him. For an instant, I thought he might run from the room, but he bowed to our guests, as awkward as any child his age.

"Be welcome," he said, sounding only a little sullen.

I waited until he settled at my feet, then refreshed the tea, handing Inae a small cup. He wouldn't drink it, but he liked to be included.

"Thank you, Inae," said Trua, inclining her head to him as Baighrid had done. She drank before speaking again and avoided meeting my eye. "I understand the difficulty of the situation. You are correct, however. We have come to take you home. You must be taught."

I didn't argue. How could I argue, when each morning I swept away the evidence of Inae's dreaming? That morning, it had been flower petals. A week prior, rabbits. Before that, thorn vines. I was still healing from the cuts. My husband's silly tales of his own misadventures in the icy cliffs of the god-touched lost their laughter when mapped onto Inae, a boy surrounded by the fragile lives of the forest and the village.

But he was my son and all I had left of the man I had loved.

"We understand, Honored One." I kept my voice level, calling upon the calm I used when dealing with the sick and injured. Hysteria would not help me lead them to feelings of contentment. For Inae's sake, they must see me as a still, shallow pool. No ripples on the surface, no depths to fear beneath.

With normal visitors, I might have pressed peace, but attempting to nudge the emotions of a god-touched was like trying to heat the ocean with warm stones. Instead, I used my minor abilities on the room, encouraging the birdsong to carry on the light breeze and touching the lavender so the sweetness of its scent filled the air with quiet welcome. The sun had not yet chased away the past night's chill, but my sitting room grew warm with drowsy summer heat.

"Mama already teaches me," said Inae, but he hushed when I squeezed his shoulder.

"The god-touched hold in the mountains, don't they?" I asked, as if we made small talk. "A long ride, that."

"Three months we've been traveling. Another month back to the Blessed Peaks." Baighrid didn't quite manage to keep the road-weariness from his voice. "A long, cold ride."

"Long winters," I said, hoping the shadow of old sympathy was enough to color my words. "Or so Inae's father used to tell me."

I had wondered, until then, if they knew. Trua's eyes, gone cold again, answered me. I shouldn't have mentioned him. Now, they would be thinking of his defection, of the secrets he might have shared with me.

"He spoke of it?" Trua threw the words like sharp, gray stones. She shifted and I could see she was ready to stand, to leave and take my Inae with her.

I didn't flinch. All was lost if I did. Instead, I handed Inae a biscuit of his own, warning him not to make a mess of things. "Of the cold, yes. And of the food, Honored One." I kept my tone light, forcing myself to think not of Inae, but of the laughter hiding in my husband's voice as he moaned about the rations he had once lived on. Not fit, he had said, for a mule.

"Ahh..." The cold melted as Trua gave her biscuit a look of pitiable longing. "Yes, that would come up. It's hard to bring fresh food so far and conjuring dinner is a waste of magic."

"Potatoes every meal if the crop is good, he said."

Baighrid, too, look pained. He took a long, indulgent sip of tea. "How I wish denials were possible."

Inae finished his biscuit and sat with his arms wrapped around himself, his eyes fixed on the ground. With any other guests, I would have reproached him. Instead, I tangled my fingers back through his hair, letting his hurt speak what I couldn't. Trua and Baighrid, I judged, had been given reminder enough of what awaited them in the mountains; their expressions were almost as storm-ridden as Inae's.

"Let us speak of closer meals," I ran a mental inventory of the larder and knew a trip to the village would be necessary. "Will you stay for supper, Honored Ones?"

The look they exchanged wrote its meaning on the air. They would have been two hours walking from the village inn, where they must have taken rooms. I knew the inn-keeper, a sour-faced, irritable man who scrimped on bedding and food alike. We had never gotten on well, but in that moment I adored him.

"We could?" Baighrid made it a question, looking to Trua for permission.

"It would be a late walk, if we did." Trua's sigh said she cared for neither walk nor inn.

"You might honor me by sleeping here, then? I have the space. A room for each of you, warded against fleas and other vermin. I fear the inn is not so well protected."

"We would have to leave at sunrise." Baighrid said, his slurring accent becoming a guilt-ridden mumble. He met my gaze but his fish hid itself in the depths of his pupil, only a bit of tailfin visible. "Inae, as well."

My hands began to shake again and I couldn't steady them. To hear it said, so bluntly, almost undid me. They planned to steal my boy at sunrise. I thought of flinging myself at Baighrid's feet, weeping. Only after the fantasy passed, and I had control of my voice again, did I speak. "I know. But if you stay, I will have the night with him, and a chance to prepare proper rations for the three of you."

"That would be well," Trua said. She didn't have Baighrid's open face or tattling fish, but I thought she agreed as much for my sake as for the promise of decent road fare. Her reasons mattered little, so long as she placed herself in my hands.

"Then we will feast tonight, and you will forgive me if I forgo the tubers to which you are accustomed."

Trua laughed, a bright, glittering noise which appeared to surprise her as much as it did me. "I almost wish we could linger here."

"You have your duties, Honored One. You must travel as need requires." I didn't mention the summer storm, days late, I could feel building in the drowsy heat. Nor did I warn them of Inae's terror of thunder, the impossibility of getting him outside when lightning cut the sky. Even if the storm broke in the night, the roads would be a misery for days.

And I would make of the house a quiet respite, all warm meals and sweet smells, while outside the storm winds howled. My magics were small, but I had never had a guest leave after only a night of visiting. Even these guests, I knew, would find reasons for delay.

When the storm broke just before dawn the next morning, they begged a day of me. The day became a week; Trua had caught a small cold. By the second week my honored guests had started courting, all longing glances and childish giggling. By the third, I moved Baighrid into Trua's room.

I kept their days easy. Very little tempts one to idleness quite like comfort. Trua took Inae on daily walks to the river and began teaching him not to fear the water. Every evening, I served a feast out in the garden, pouring wine as the deer came in from the forest to nibble Inae's curls and lie in Trua's lap.

On the fourth week, when Baighrid shyly asked if he might plant a few things among my herbs, I knew they would stay. No safety in that. Others would come. Hadn't they hounded my husband?

When Josen arrived, black-robed and dark-eyed, I feared myself beaten. He ate little, spoke less, and scowled at Baighrid and Trua. Only my Inae, who took to following him like deer followed Trua, claimed his smile. The man was a natural teacher, and my son has always been eager to learn. Inae worshipped him, agreed with everything he said, including the importance of returning to the mountains. After a particularly trying morning, spent chasing the venomous snakes Inae had dreamed, I watched the two of them together and thought of loosing my grip.

"He does not teach, on the mountain," Baighrid said, coming to stand beside me. "Young men aren't permitted such duties. He sees to the health of the yaks."

None of my magics had reached the man. But my son, who I sent running to Josen with even his smallest questions, did. Within two weeks, Inae's dream magics were under control and my newest resident no longer spoke of taking my son away. Instead, he confessed a love for apple dumplings. I began to bake them nightly.

The following month, two more arrived. We had to expand the cottage, an easy task with so many god-touched to assist. Three weeks later we expanded it again, after Baighrid announced he had invited 'a few colleagues to visit'. With so many now gathering, I would need to arrange some further distractions.

I found the answer while watching them bicker over time with Inae. They all had knowledge to share and only one child to share it with. But I had heard rumors of other god-touched children, fathered by men of dazzling power and little responsibility. Some mothers called for the god-touched as soon as such a child was born. But others, well, I knew what it was to live as they did. Fearing every magical disruption would bring the god-touched knocking.

They would be desperate, as I had been desperate. It was a simple thing, to spread the rumor of a safe place. A few words to Lord and Lady Aride, a few more in the village commons, where the traveling merchants gathered. Soon enough, the families came to the village, and the children came to my door.

Inae was delighted at the new playmates. First a pair of twins, then a southern girl, then a shy boy who clung to Inae like a shadow.

They grew so quickly, my boy and his new friends. Not locked in some mountain stronghold, but playing tag through sun-dappled forests, making friends with foxes, and getting into trouble with the village children.

The god-touched taught them to twist the very weave of the world. I taught them the best herbs for a broken heart, and how to brew a perfect cup of tea. I made the school their home.

How easy it was, to imagine it would always be that way. Children trickling in, finding safety, and my Inae in the thick of them, part of the great unruly family I'd created to keep him safe.

But home, for a child, feels a cage to a youth. It's fourteen years since Trua and Baighrid came to my door, and my Inae has all the wanderlust his age implies. He's planned a grand tour of the three kingdoms and speaks of establishing a new school in the Southlands. He doesn't speak of returning home.

What can a mother do when faced with such eager abandonment?

Smile. Pack his travel rations carefully. And hope. Somewhere, a brave, warm-eyed girl is blending tea with a whisper of magic. She'll find a way to bring him to her door.

And he'll find reason to linger.

"Small Magics" originally appeared in *Metaphorosis* on Friday, 17 June 2016.

About the author

Kelly Sandoval's fiction has appeared in *Uncanny*, *Strange Horizons*, and *Asimov's*. She lives in Seattle, where the weather is always happy to make staying in and writing seem like a good idea. In her nonexistent free time, she's an editor at *Liminal Stories*. Her family includes a patient husband, three unruly cats, and an anarchist tortoise.

You can find out more at kellysandovalfiction.com and follow her on Twitter at @kellymsandoval

Copyright

Authors also retain copyrights to all other material in
the anthology.

<u>First appearance</u>

All stories first appeared in *Metaphorosis,* except

"Images Across a Shattered Sea" first appeared in
    Writers of the Future, Volume 32
"Daughter of the Sea" first appeared in *Truancy*
"Lift Up Your Cores, O Ye Ships" first appeared in the
    Night Lights anthology
"May Dreams Shelter Us" first appeared in *Diabolical
    Plots*
"Closed Circuit" first appeared in *Plasma Frequency*

Metaphorosis Publishing

Metaphorosis offers beautifully written science fiction and fantasy. Our imprints include:

Metaphorosis Magazine

Plant Based Press

Metaphorosis Books

Driftwyrd

Vestige

See more about some of our books on the following pages.

Metaphorosis

a magazine of speculative fiction

Metaphorosis is a weekly science fiction and fantasy magazine. Find out more at magazine.metaphorosis.com, and sign up to be notified when new stories come out every Friday.

We also publish monthly print and e-book issues, as well as yearly Best of and Complete anthologies.

**Metaphorosis:
Best of 2018**

The best science fiction and fantasy stories from *Metaphorosis* magazine's third year.

Metaphorosis 2018

All the stories from *Metaphorosis* magazine's third year. Fifty-two great SFF stories.

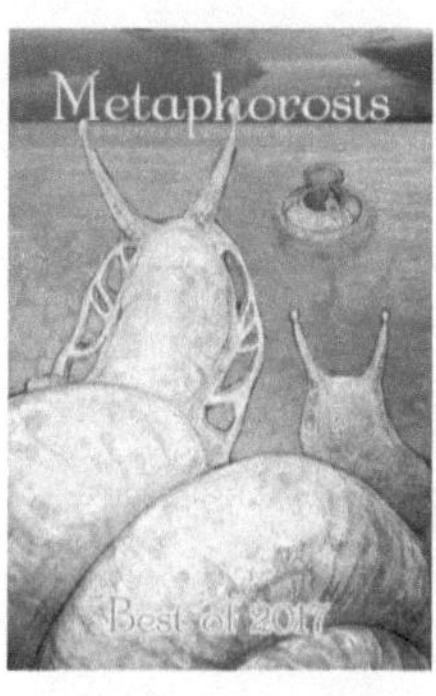

Metaphorosis:
Best of 2017

The best science fiction
and fantasy stories from
Metaphorosis magazine's
second year.

Metaphorosis 2017

All the stories from
Metaphorosis magazine's
second year. Fifty-three
great SFF stories.

Metaphorosis:
Best of 2016

The best science fiction
and fantasy stories from
Metaphorosis magazine's
first year.

Metaphorosis 2016

Almost all the stories from
Metaphorosis magazine's
first year.

Plant Based Press

Vegan-friendly science fiction and fantasy, including an annual anthology of the year's best SFF stories.

Best Vegan SFF of 2018

The best vegan science fiction and fantasy stories of 2018!

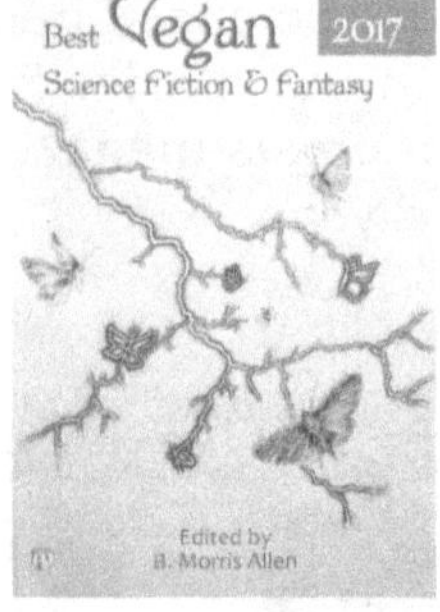

Best Vegan SFF of 2017

The best vegan science fiction and fantasy stories of 2017!

**Best Vegan SFF
of 2016**

The best vegan science
fiction and fantasy stories of
2016!

Susurrus

A darkly romantic story of
magic, love, and suffering.

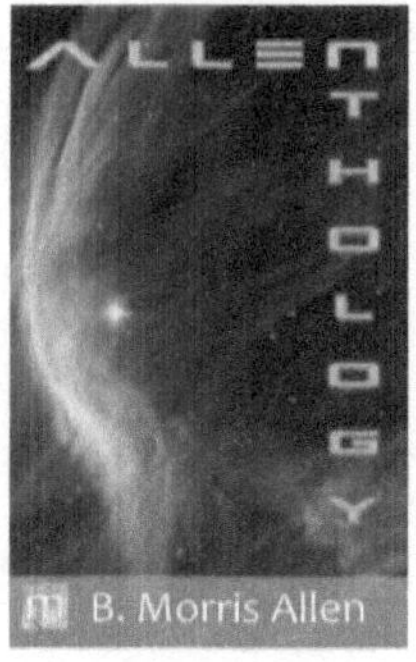

**Allenthology:
Volume I**

A quarter century of SFF
stories, including the full
contents of the collections
Tocsin, Start with Stones,
and *Metaphorosis.*

Metaphorosis Books

Science fiction and fantasy books for writers – full of great stories, but with an additional focus on the craft of speculative fiction writing.

Score

an SFF symphony

What if stories were written like music? *Score* is an anthology of varied stories arranged to follow an emotional score from the heights of joy to the depths of despair – but always with a little hope shining through.

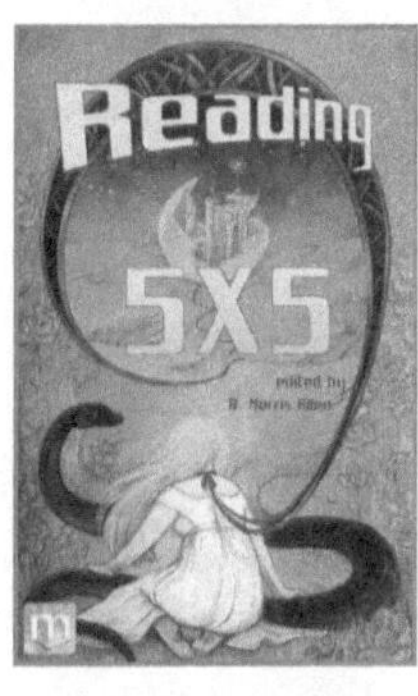

Reading 5X5

Five stories, five times

Twenty-five SFF authors, five base stories, five versions of each – see how different writers take on the same material, with stories in contemporary and high fantasy, soft and hard SF, and a mysterious 'other' category.

Reading 5X5

Writers' Edition

All the stories from the regular, readers' edition, plus two extra stories, the story seed, and authors' notes on writing. Over 100 pages of additional material specifically aimed at writers.